WOMAN, RUNNING LATE, IN A DRESS

Stories by Dallas Woodburn

~ The Cypress & Pine Fiction Series ~

WOMAN, RUNNING LATE, IN A DRESS
Dallas Woodburn

All Stories © Dallas Woodburn
© 2018 Yellow Flag Press

Cover art by © Beatrice Murch
Author photo by Jeffrey Dransfeldt
Layout and Design by W. Scott Thomason

First Edition
March 2018

ISBN 978-1-387-57121-5

Yellow Flag Press

www.yellowflagpress.com

YFP-146

Praise for *Woman, Running Late, in a Dress*

"Dallas Woodburn's collection of interwoven stories shows real maturity about the complexities of relationships of all kinds, and she doesn't shirk from the painful experiences of her characters. Even so, the writing is so lively and the scenes so engaging that the reader gets to move fluidly between heft and lightness. A terrific debut!"
– Aimee Bender, author of *The Color Master*

"Dallas Woodburn's *Woman, Running Late, in a Dress* is a stunning collection, its stories full of tragedy and grace in equal measure. Deeply moving."
– Vanessa Hua, author of *A River of Stars*

"Dallas Woodburn's *Woman, Running Late, in a Dress* is striking for its formal range and its fresh take on the old subjects — love, death, and the death of love, yearning and loss in all their varieties. There's nothing predictable here. No neat epiphanies or easy-to-diagram plots. These stories blaze their own trails. The characters are core optimists dealing, for the first time or all over again, with the tragedy of the world. Your heart will go out to them, and to this extraordinary debut collection."
– Porter Shreve, author of *The End of the Book*

"Dallas Woodburn writes with rare insight and compassion about the aching glory of being young. These skillfully connected stories still resonate long after they're read."
– Hilma Wolitzer, author of *An Available Man*

Contents

Woman, Running Late, in a Dress

For my parents, who give me roots and wings; Greg, who teaches me patience and faith, and to find joy in the journey; and Allyn, who holds my hand, my constant through it all.

And in memory of Céline Lucie Aziz, who I miss every day, and who wore the most fabulous dresses in all colors of the rainbow.

Near-Death Experience

What happened was, William had a stroke. A mild one, the doctor said. But he was out for a few minutes. I found him in the living room, collapsed beside my bag of knitting, his cheek against the carpet, the television blaring Larry King. The window was open; from outside came the rumbling of a truck, the laughter of the children next door playing in their front yard. It was an early autumn evening, hot and dry from the Santa Ana winds. The breeze coming in through the window offered no relief from the stifling heaviness in the air.

Of course I was scared when I saw William like that. Of course my heart started beating fast and I ran over to my husband and stroked his face and tried to wake him. Of course I called 9-1-1 and cried into the phone for an ambulance.

Later, when I sat beside William's hospital bed and he reached over and squeezed my hand and smiled, I felt relief like none I'd ever felt before. That I wasn't alone in this world. That he hadn't left me yet.

But then he came home from the hospital, and he started going on and on about God and Jesus and being "saved" and "seeing the light." At first I thought it was just a phase, just something he had to get out of his system. But it's been four months now, and if anything he's just getting more belligerent about it. He wants me to go to church with him. He wants the two of us to get baptized together. He keeps a Bible on the nightstand and reads passages out loud before bed, like a preacher in a movie. I always roll over and pretend to be asleep. Any response from me would just encourage him, make him dig in his heels even more. William is stubborn as the waves crashing onto the beach, breaking rocks down into sand.

"Did you pray for me?" William asks.

7

We're sitting at the breakfast table, sunlight peeping in through the thin yellow curtains. It's the first week of October. Overnight, it seems, the summer warmth has been wiped from the air. I'm taking a gardening class at the community college – *Eat Your Own Home-Grown Vegetables This Winter!* the course listing promised, which made me think of the Laura Ingalls Wilder books my mother read to me as a girl. When I signed up for the course, it was my mother I thought of. She's been dead for years, yet still I find myself ranking my actions on her scale of approval or disapproval.

Today, a Saturday, I will plant my vegetables. I'm drinking ginger tea and eating warm toast with jam and thinking about my new trowel and sunhat and the feel of moist soil between my fingers. And then William has to ruin the moment with his talking.

"When I was in the ambulance?" he persists. "Did you pray for me?"

I sip my tea and stare at the curtains, trying to glimpse images in the folds of the cloth and the patterns of light shining through. There's a jacaranda tree right outside the kitchen window, in the side yard, and its branches cast shadows onto the sunlit yellow. William planted that tree shortly after we moved into this house. We were newlyweds then. We put a lot of effort into sprucing up this place – painting things, planting things, buying things. Trying to make this house ours. Trying to turn it into a home.

I remember how strong William seemed to me then. He is not a tall man, but he has broad shoulders and back then he stood very straight, his chin lifted up a little when he talked, which made him seem taller than he was. Sometimes, when he hugged me close, he gripped me so tight it hurt. To be honest, I liked the helplessness he brought out in me. It was what drew me to him from the beginning. It was what made me marry him. The belief he would take care of me, yes. That he would provide a good life for me and for our future children. But more than a promise of security, I think I was attracted to a recklessness I sensed in William, a hint of danger in his strength – the knowledge that, if he wanted to, he could pick me up and carry me off somewhere, anywhere he pleased, and there was nothing I could do about it.

After he planted that jacaranda tree outside our kitchen window, William was jubilant. It was just a sapling, with small leaves poking out tentatively from thin branches, but William was taken with the idea of it. "This will grow into the tallest tree on the block," he said, kissing me, his hands leaving smudges of dirt on my face. "Just wait and see. Someday our kids will climb this tree. I'll build a tree house for them to play in. How's that sound?"

"Wonderful," I said, pressing my cheek against his, kissing his neck. Back then, I wanted a houseful of children. I thought children were like geese and we would have a gaggle of them.

"Sylvie?" William says, bringing me back to the present. He places his hand on the table, beside my cup. He could reach over, just so, and graze my wrist with his index finger. If he wanted to. But he hasn't touched me since his stroke.

"Did you pray for me?" he asks, a new urgency in his voice.

I could get up and walk out of the room. Walk right past him into the living room, upstairs to the bedroom, and close the door. I could walk around the kitchen table and out the sliding glass door and into the garden, pulling my housecoat around my waist against the dewy morning chill. I could stay right where I am and reach for the newspaper, unfold it slowly, study the smudgy print, and act like I don't hear him. Ignore him and ignore him and ignore him no matter how many times he asks.

But I don't do any of these things. I tilt my face up to meet William's grey-green eyes, filled with a new earnestness. I ask, "What do you mean by pray?"

When William was taken away in the ambulance, of course I thought, *Please let him be okay.* Words ran through my brain like charms. *Oh Dear God Oh Dear God.* Words crammed my brain, the same words over and over, squeezing out all other thought until I was left silently chanting: *Please please please please please.* Sitting alone in the corner of a hospital waiting room, fingers rubbing back and forth over the rubbery waxen leaf of a fake plant on the magazine table, waiting for the doctor to come back and tell me something. *Pleasep Leasepl Easeple Aseplease.* I want to ask William, *Did you know that when you say a word too many times, its edges begin to bleed together until it loses all meaning?*

       Is that what praying is?

       "Did you ask God to save me?" William asks, scooting his chair closer to mine. "When I was taken away in the ambulance, did you ask Him to grant me more time here on Earth with you?"

       The absurdity of hearing this type of language come out of William's mouth causes my body to tighten, as if shielding itself from impending hurt. My hands clench around my mug of tea. I can hear it in William's voice – he's not saying him, he's saying Him. Upper case. *Did you ask Him to save me?* I want to say, "Okay, you can stop the act. You got me good. But that's enough, all right? Enough now."

       Instead, I laugh. I can't help it.

       William frowns at me, then pushes his chair back and leaves the room.

       I started taking classes at the community college after I learned I could not have children. To ease the gnawing emptiness of my womb, I took up pottery, basket-weaving, knitting, quilting. I stuffed myself with facts about World War II, the French Revolution, Imperialist Japan; I studied French for two semesters, imagining a trip to Paris with William, walking arm-in-arm along the boulevards and sampling wine in the sidewalk cafes. But then William lost his job for drinking too much at the office holiday party and kissing the boss's wife. I was not there. The dental office where I work had its own holiday party that night, and I was hanging up garlands of fake pine when I got the phone call from William asking if I could come pick him up. In the weeks following – the marriage counseling, the Alcoholics Anonymous meetings, the tears and accusations, the night I threw a wine glass and cut William's forehead so deep he needed stitches – I stopped going to French class and threw away the Paris brochures I'd bought. The make-up sex made me feel like I was hurtling towards life and death in one simultaneous dizzying blur.

The only person I told about William's indiscretion was Carol, a fellow Midwest transplant who I met Photography 101; we've taken a class together every semester since. Carol and I became friends because neither of us has children. Other women our age are always talking about their children, and there's only so much a person can take.

Carol does not mince words. "Sylvie, listen to me," she said when I told her why William lost his job. "He's never gonna change."

But Carol wouldn't understand – she married a surgeon. Raymond. Steady, reliable, nice-guy Raymond. I knew Carol and Raymond didn't love each other the way William and I did. A love wrapped up in need. Because William did – he *needed* me. He told me nearly every day and it was exhilarating to hear, like the catch I heard in his breath when I climbed on top of him and held his wrists against the bed, knowing in that moment I was the only one who could give him what he wanted. He was trying to sober up – very hard, he was trying – but he would never be able to do it without me there. He said this and I knew I could not leave him.

When I get home from work, William's sitting on the couch – sitting very close on the couch – beside Alice Townsend from two doors down. They seem deep in conversation, but both look up when they see me come in.

"Sylvie!" William says, as if I've been gone three weeks.

"Hi, Sylvie," Alice says, scooting ever-so-slightly away from William. "I just stopped by to see how you two are getting along." She's a russet-haired young mother of twin boys. Her legs are longer than a flamingo's and she's wearing shorts. She's the only mother I know who can get away with wearing shorts. "I'm so glad this guy is doing okay." She pats William's knee, once.

There was a time that coming home to a scene like this would have made me intensely jealous. Worries about William leaving me would flit around my mind constantly, keeping me awake at night, making me jittery and forgetful during the day so I'd get people's appointments mixed up and double-booked. Eventually I would collapse into tears, and William would get frustrated and tired of "talking in circles about the same damn thing." He'd storm out and come home drunk and I'd wake up to his large hands on my thighs, his lips kissing my neck, his breath warm and insistent with apology. Afterwards, I'd nestle into him and we'd both sleep like the babies we'd never have. In the morning, my worries would start up again.

But that was years ago. Now, he's telling Alice Townsend about the instant before his stroke, when – "for no reason I can explain," he says, "it wasn't a commercial or anything" – he glanced away from Larry King on the TV and felt his eyes drawn towards my bag of knitting on the floor beside his favorite armchair. A royal blue ball of yarn was poised at the top of the bag, for a sweater I'm knitting for Carol, whose favorite color is blue and whose birthday is next month. In the weave and fray of the ball of yarn, in the shadows playing across its surface from the glowing side table lamp, in that instant before his stroke William swears he saw the face of Jesus.

"And I thought, *Jesus, you are my savior and I love you*," William says, taking Alice's hands in his own and gazing her full in the face. "And I felt this warmth through my entire body." He pauses for even more dramatic effect. "And I knew, right then, that everything was going to be all right."

He lets out a big breath of air, and so does Alice, and I watch them smiling at each other. Alice wipes away a tear from the corner of her eye. Ever since William came home from the hospital, when I've witnessed moments like this between my husband and someone else, I want to be different. I want to be someone like Alice. Someone who can share that with William – a feeling of awe, giddiness, triumph at his salvation. But I don't believe that Jesus really appeared before my husband in a ball of yarn in my knitting bag. I've pretended a lot of things since I married William, but I can't pretend to feel that.

Last summer, before William's stroke, Carol and I signed up for a poetry course and read Yeats' poem "Leda and the Swan." It made me think of William. *Her thighs caressed / By the dark webs, her nape caught in his bill / He holds her helpless breast upon his breast.* Our teacher spoke about the classical myth the poem was based upon, where the Greek god Zeus takes the form of a swan and seduces Leda.

"This isn't seduction," Carol said, holding up her photocopied handout of the poem. "This is rape. The swan is raping Leda."

To my surprise, the teacher agreed. The entire class agreed. I nodded along, because I didn't know what else to do. I wasn't about to raise my hand and ask, *Am I the only one who thinks this is a sexy poem? That maybe the swan loves Leda, loves her so much he can't stand to be without her?*

On my first date with William, he ordered beer after beer all through dinner – he must have downed five brimming pint glasses by the time we were finished with our meal. I don't remember what I ordered or what we talked about. Mostly I remember the dark brown walls, the glass-topped tables, the way the pint glasses left rings of moisture, a mosaic of wet smeary circles. I remember the way William grinned at me, winking as he said to the waitress, "Yeah, I suppose I'll have one more." And the waitress would come back with another foamy glass, not batting an eye, calmly refilling my iced tea as she set the beer down in front of William.

The thing about William was, he did not seem inebriated. He did not slur his words or speak too loudly or tell off-color jokes. He was charming and fun and he looked me as if he had been waiting his entire life to bask in the glory of my presence. He said I looked beautiful. I was wearing a red dress with a sweetheart neckline and a wide purple belt I'd found at a thrift store. I thought William was unspeakably handsome. I thought it was sophisticated and manly, the way he was able to hold down all that liquor without seeming drunk. I was twenty-two years old, new in town, infatuated with the beach and the sunshine and the freedom of living halfway across the country from everything I'd grown up knowing. I had a part-time job as a secretary at a small dental office. Nights and weekends, I painted cartoonish landscapes of cornfields and farmhouses in fluorescent colors. I gathered sand from the beach and mixed it into my paint for texture; I decorated my bedroom with seashells and driftwood. I saw myself as a daring artist living the grand *bohème* life.

But I was lonely. My only friends were Suzette, the 52-year-old dental hygienist who worked afternoons at the office, and a girl named Jo-Ann who had been sorority sisters with my high school friend Charlene's cousin, and who I occasionally met for coffee before work even though we didn't have much to say to each other than analyzing what had happened on *Dynasty* that week. My typical Friday evenings, before William leaned in through the glass partition separating me from the dental office waiting room and asked if I was free for dinner sometime, usually consisted of peanut-butter-and-banana sandwiches, halfhearted pencil sketches in my notebook, and falling asleep to Johnny Carson. After three weeks of dinners and drinks, when I finally caved in and slept with William for the first time – on a blanket in the sand dunes at midnight, ocean waves murmuring on the edges of my consciousness – I was sure I would never see him again.

But William surprised me. He kept calling and coming around, and within a year he asked me to marry him. At our wedding reception, he was a little over the edge of tipsy into drunk. No one else seemed to mind, or perhaps they didn't notice. Even sober, William was one of those loud, flamboyant guys who liked to be the center of attention. His flushed cheeks and crazed dance moves could very well have been the uncorked energy of a happy groom about to embark on his honeymoon. But I knew William, and I could tell he was drunk. When we slow-danced together, he pinched my bottom and kissed my ear wetly, sloppily. His breath smelled of bourbon. "I love you," he said, and it made my heart sink because I loved him, too, and deep down I knew in a vague, bleary way that perhaps William needing to binge on alcohol meant that something in his life was missing. That something between us was missing. But these thoughts happened in a place of my brain that was easy to push away and ignore. And so I did. For years and years, I did.

How can those terrified vague fingers push / The feathered glory from her loosening thighs? / And how can body, laid in that white rush / But feel the strange heart beating where it lies?

That day last summer, I arrived home from poetry class, opened the front door and called a hello to William. There was no answer. I found him unconscious in the living room, the television blaring Larry King, the laughter of Alice Townsend's children floating in through the open window.

Ever since his stroke, William has not touched a drop of liquor. He has not sipped a single beer. He hasn't even thrown them out – the cans remain in our fridge, couched between the jar of mayonnaise and carton of milk. The whiskey and gin and rum bottles glisten in the cabinet beside the stove. It is as if William relishes the temptation – the knowledge that he is living purely in a house full of sin. Or perhaps he is so confident in this new salvation he has found, this new self he is trying on, that he does not even feel tempted.

15

Since I will not go to church with him, William invites some of his church friends over for dinner. He asks me to make spaghetti. "Your famous spaghetti," he says. "Everyone loves your famous spaghetti."

According to William, my mother made the best spaghetti sauce he ever tasted. My spaghetti came in second – "a distant second," he once said, after a few glasses of wine. He must have seen the hurt on my face, because he immediately tried to take it back. "I'm kidding!" he shouted, grabbing my arm as I turned away from the table and tried to stand up. He pulled me down into his lap. "I'm only kidding," he said again, taking a sloppy bite of spaghetti off his fork, sauce flecking his face with red. He wiped his cheek against mine, and his whiskers grated like sandpaper. "You take everything too seriously," he said.

"Sorry," I said. Somehow I was always the one apologizing. If you had asked me, I wouldn't have been able to articulate what I was apologizing for.

I agree to make spaghetti for William's new friends. As I dump the box of brittle noodles into the boiling water, I think of my mother in her hot kitchen in the summertime, rolling out thin strands of pasta dough on the cool marble slab she kept beside the sink. She spent hours in that kitchen. She said she enjoyed cooking for her family. Mostly, though, I think she was cooking for my father, trying to impress him, or at least please him. My father, with his thick gray mustache and unsmiling eyes, never said one nice thing about my mother's cooking. Or, if he did, I never heard it. After she died, he threw away all her cooking supplies, married a blonde twice-divorced D-cup named Linda, and moved to Florida like a tired cliché.

Tonight, I don't have the energy. I don't care what these church people think of my cooking. I take another pot down from its hook above the stove, pop open a jar of Prego, and pour.

They arrive bearing sparkling cider and wide smiles: Rick and Suzanne, Jack and Margaret. Before his stroke, William was never much of a hugger, but now I watch him hug each person before ushering them inside. His new friends. His people.

I place the cider on the table, along with a bottle of white wine. Jack and Margaret exchange a look.

Suzanne leans close, her hand on my arm. "You must be so proud of Liam," she says.

Liam? William's grandfather was Irish, but he's never wanted to go by anything but William. He doesn't even like me to call him Will.

"How long has it been now?" Jack asks.

"Almost six months," William says, beaming. "And you know what? I don't even miss it."

"That's wonderful, honey." I try to make my smile natural. "You know I'm proud of you." And I am. How long have I wished and wished for William to drink less? How many nights have I worried about him driving home? Still, I can't help but feel insulted. Cast aside. I've spent every year of our marriage trying everything I can think of to help him sober up, and nothing has ever worked for long. Now all of a sudden he's "found the light" and he's quit cold turkey, just like that?

Rick and Suzanne, Jack and Margaret – how are these people enough for him when I have never been enough?

Without looking at William, I pick up the bottle of wine. It feels damp under my fingers, moisture beading in the warmth of the room. The bottle is full, heavy. A weapon. I tilt the lip against my glass and pour.

"Cheers!" I toast the room. "You don't mind, do you, William?"

"Of course not," he says. I search for tension in his eyes, his smile, the set of his jaw, but he looks relaxed, happy. Peaceful.

Over dinner, Jack tells a story about when he and Margaret went to Israel and Margaret took a trip to

17

Bethlehem by herself. "I was in meetings all day," Jack says. I seem to have missed what his meetings were about, but he's ploughing on, talking about how dangerous Bethlehem is these days, especially for Americans and women. I pour myself another glass of wine. Jack smiles at Margaret like she is a puppy that stole a sock from the dryer. "I knew my girl would be all right," he says. "I knew it was something she had to do."

Margaret nods. "It's the Holy City," she says. "I had to go there. I had to."

"You know, I wasn't even worried," Jack says. "Because I knew someone up there was looking after her and He wouldn't let any harm come to my girl."

Everyone around the table is smiling, but I feel anger rising within me, a warm steady burning. I take another sip of wine. *See, this is what I don't like about you people*, I want to say. *You're so sure God is looking after you — that you can do reckless, senseless things and still be safe from harm.*

I take another sip of wine. A big sip, more like a gulp.

Everyone who dies — it's like you're saying that God wasn't watching over them, that he doesn't care about them. Don't you see how damn self-righteous you're being?

"Sylvie, please!" William says, his face pained. Everyone is looking at me with round surprised eyes and I realize with a sharp ache that I've said this last part out loud.

It's all William's fault. These are not my people. This house does not feel like mine with them here. This can't be the same dining room William and I painted all those years ago, newlyweds with a big can of barn-red paint, carefully maneuvering our brushes along the baseboards and crown molding in the corners.

How did I get here? How did we get here?

"I'm — excuse me for a minute," I say, stumbling out of my chair, standing up and pushing it back into place. "I'll just be upstairs. William, there's cobbler on the counter and ice cream in the fridge for dessert. I mean the freezer — there's ice cream in the freezer." And I flee.

There's something I've never told anyone, not even William. When I gave birth to Hannah, I died. I left my body and felt myself hovering over everything. I looked down at the small bright room, at my own body in the hospital bed, at the ring of doctors and nurses surrounding me with their charts and instruments, at William, pacing along the back wall, alarm evident on his face – and, despite all the signs to the contrary, I felt an overwhelming sense of peace. I knew, with more conviction than I've had about anything before or since, that everything would be all right. Hannah would be okay. I would be okay. He, up there, was watching over us.

The next thing I knew, I was waking up in a different hospital room. William was sitting on a chair beside my bed, looking out the window. I said his name and he turned to me, and I saw it right there on his face.

In that moment, I stopped believing in God.

What I want to tell William – what I want to tell everyone downstairs, throat-clearing their way through peach cobbler and coffee – is what I know to be true. Salvation is smoke and mirrors, a comforter we wrap around ourselves and hug close to keep from going crazy. Because if there was a God, he would not have let it happen the way it did. Not only losing Hannah, but not being able to have any children, ever? Nothing to hang on to, nothing to hope for, nothing to even begin to fill the emptiness? I couldn't paint anymore. Anytime I tried, I would end up staring at the blank canvas for hours. I burned the last painting I had been working on – a calm, moonlit ocean for Hannah's baby room – and threw the rest of my paints and supplies away.

"The world is a cruel place," I say softly. And then, because it feels good, I say it again louder, almost shouting. For a few moments I wait for the rhythm of William's footsteps on the stairs, coming to soothe or reprimand, but the low murmur of voices from downstairs is uninterrupted.

Head pounding, I lie down on top of the bed William and I share, on top of the quilt I sewed in that maw of grief that was my life after losing Hannah. The quilt is made out of scraps from my maternity shirts and William's blue jeans. I sewed the entire thing by hand because I couldn't bear the noise of the sewing machine.

Lying on top of the covers makes me feel raw and exposed. Even in the summertime, I lie underneath a sheet. In the early years of our marriage, William and I would sleep naked, curled against each other, skin warming bare skin. Now, I unhook my bra and turn on my side. A bobby pin digs into my scalp but I don't have the energy to remove it.

Later tonight, William will wave goodbye to our guests from the front porch. He will rinse the dishes and put them in the dishwasher. He will spoon the leftover pasta into a plastic container, and the sauce into its own separate container, and when I open the fridge in the morning to get milk for my coffee the two containers will be there, stacked neatly on top of one another. He will step gently, quietly, upstairs and look in on me, sleeping. My mouth will most likely be open, snoring drool onto the pillowcase. William will unfold a blanket and drape it over me. I will not wake up. I am a heavy sleeper, especially with the wine. He will sleep on the couch downstairs, waking up early because tomorrow is Sunday, and he goes to the 8 a.m. sermon and then out to breakfast with his church friends.

I want to open my eyes in the middle of the night and feel his body curled around mine. He once held me for three days, rocking back and forth in this great big bed as I cried and stared emptily at the walls.

On our first date, William drove me home. Looking back, I am sure he was too drunk to drive, but that night I wasn't worried. He opened the car door for me and I climbed inside without a second thought. I was twenty-two years old, wearing a red dress with a sweetheart neckline, on my first date with a man who looked into my eyes as if he was searching for salvation and I was the only one in the world who could give it to him. He drove with the windows down and radio turned low. Everywhere was the sound of the ocean. If his car veered to one side of the road and then the other, I didn't notice. He may have driven too fast, but I didn't care. The air against my face was cool and smelled of salt. I closed my eyes and thought, *Thank you.* I was willing to go wherever he would take me. I was sure we would make it there safe, together. I was sure it would be somewhere nice.

Numb

Soon after, I notice while washing my face in the shower that the palms of my hands have a new texture, rough and bumpy. I turn off the water, squeeze drops from my hair, and step out of the tub. I wipe my face with a towel and peer at my hands. The palms are criss-crossed with dozens of lines, like the skin of an old woman. My fingertips normally get prune-y if I stay in the shower too long. But I took a quick shower, not even bothering to shave my legs, and both of my palms are wizened, scrunched-up prunes.

"Your hands have no oil glands," Dr. Anderson says over the phone. I've known her a dozen years – we went to high school together – but she's using her Nonchalant Doctor Tone. It turns me into a patient, just one of many patients; it makes her seem like a stranger. "No oil glands means your skin expands and prunes up," she explains.

"So there is something wrong with me?"

"Beg pardon?"

"You're saying my hands are supposed to have oil glands?"

"No, no, everyone's hands are like that. It's nothing to worry about."

"Oh." I gently rub my thumb across the alligatored texture. Already the pruneiness is melting away; they are turning back into regular palms. I feel foolish. "Sorry to bother you, Val," I say. "I just thought it was strange."

"It's no bother – I'm glad you called." Her voice softens. "How you holding up?"

"Fine, I'm doing fine. Thanks."

The next morning, I wake up and my right hand is pins-and-needles-y. "I must have slept on it wrong," I tell Frank. We sit across from each other at the breakfast table, with our Cheerios and coffee, reading the newspaper to avoid eye contact. I massage my right hand with my left, gently squeezing each fingertip. My nails turn a brief white as my fingers press down, then immediately flood with pink as the pressure is released.

"Do you want me to rub it?" Frank asks. But I'm already half up out of my chair, carrying my bowl and mug to the sink. "Oh, no, it's okay," I say. I don't want him touching me.

That day, I was exhausted. The bathwater felt warm and soothing on my bare skin. Laura was napping in her nursery across the hall. I didn't fall asleep. My eyes were closed, but my ears were not. I would have heard her crying.

She didn't cry. She didn't, or I would have heard.

The tingling has spread to my toes. I sit next to Frank on the couch, prop my feet up on the coffee table, wiggle my toes in my socks. I watch them move, but it is like they are someone else's toes.

Frank sets down the latest issue of *Golf Digest* and meets my eyes. His hair is sticking up like tufts of dead brown grass. "Call the doctor," he says.

"But I just called her a couple days ago. She said it's nothing to worry about."

Frank reaches for my hand. I let him hold it for a minute, then I squeeze his hand and pull mine away. I stand up.

"Evie," Frank says, "Do you think..." He pauses.

I am already walking away, into the living room, so I pretend not to hear. He doesn't finish the sentence.

Laura was sixteen months, three weeks, and five days old. I said she had Frank's blue eyes; Frank said she had mine. She was beautiful. When I held her, she would nuzzle her face into my neck and I could feel her soft eyelashes blinking against my skin.

The numbness has spread from my hands up my forearms, past my elbows, all the way to my shoulders. My limbs are dead weight.

Dr. Anderson requests a blood test. I might have diabetes, a thyroid problem, lyme disease. The nurse tells me to squeeze a foam ball and taps on my arm, searching for a vein to mine. "You should drink more water," she scolds.

"I inherited my mother's veins," I tell her. "They're naturally small. I'm sorry." I think of Laura's tiny veins, blue beneath her translucent baby skin. The nurse misses my vein the first time, but I don't feel the prick of the needle.

The blood tests come back normal. Meanwhile, the numbness continues to spread from my toes, enveloping my feet, my ankles, my shins, surrounding my knees, inching up my thighs. Dr. Anderson sends me to Dr. Sampson, a neurologist, who tapes electrodes to my legs and arms and sends jolts of electricity through my numb body.

"Yep," he murmurs, "that's right, good," as my limbs jerk on the examining table. I feel like a marionette puppet. "Everything looks normal," the neurologist says.

On the wall, beside his diploma from medical school, he has a picture of a little boy with light brown hair and freckles. "That's my son, Jared," he says, following my gaze. "Kids," he sighs. "They grow up so fast, don't they?"

My smile feels like a grimace. "Yes," I say. "They sure do."

It is midafternoon when I arrive home, the sun slanting through the bare-limbed winter trees, already close to setting. I run the bathwater, clenching and unclenching my hands underneath the warm spray from the tap. After a few moments I climb into the tub. The water steadily rises, slowly covering my goose-pimpled legs and stomach. I bend my knees so they are two islands; I lay my head back and look at the ceiling. It was just like this. The water is loud, roaring into the tub, but not so loud that I wouldn't have heard her crying.

That day, I was exhausted. I leaned my head back and closed my eyes. When I woke up, the warmth had faded from the bathwater. Still, I wasn't alarmed. I hadn't been away more than twenty or thirty minutes. I slowly toweled myself dry, slipped into a T-shirt and sweatpants, and tip-toed into Laura's nursery. She was asleep.

The bathwater rises higher and higher, creeping up my arms, covering my breasts. My palms are wrinkled prunes, like they were that day when I climbed from the bath. Now, I take a deep breath and let my head sink under the water.

That day, I bent down and kissed Laura's forehead. And then, everything shifted, like in a dream when you suddenly realize something is off – the house you are in is not your house, your bed is in the wrong place, your car out front is a different color and model than it's supposed to be. It was as if my entire life up to that moment, up to that single kiss upon my daughter's forehead, was the weight of an elephant balancing on the head of a pushpin. The balance shifted, and everything came down in a colossal violent tumbling when I realized Laura was not breathing.

Underwater, I feel the pressure building inside me. I come up gasping for breath, clutching my numbness around me like a threadbare baby's blanket.

Snow World

Katie awoke with slivers of excitement sparking in her belly like Christmas tree lights. It was the third Saturday of the month, which meant her father pulled into the driveway at noon to sweep Katie and Scotty into his orbit. He walked up to the front door as he always did, signifying his presence with his clomping workboots and smoker's cough. As always, Scotty yanked open the front door before their father pressed the doorbell. "Dad, Dad, come look at our tree!" Scotty reached for his hand, dragging him towards the living room.

"Wait just a second, bud – let me say hi to your sister first." He bent down and gave Katie a hug, the brim of his frayed Dodgers cap bumping against her head. Katie hugged him tightly and breathed him in – smoke, aftershave, chewing gum, *Dad*. He pulled away and gently tugged her ponytail. Tug, tug. His hello ritual. "You're taller every time I see you," he said. Katie smiled, pride and sadness mingling inside. Her father used to mark her height with pencil on the door of the downstairs bathroom.

"Da-ad! Dad, come look!" Scotty whined, tugging their father's hand. Katie followed them into the living room. The Christmas tree sparkled in the corner, the shiny red and purple and blue orbs their mother had bought gleaming like something in a play. What Katie thought about as the Real ornaments, the pre-divorce ornaments, had been destroyed by rats in the garage a few months before. The corners of the box were chewed through and what looked like little black grains of rice were scattered across the cold cement floor. Their mother had shrieked and told Katie and Scotty to go back inside, and the next day an exterminator came and set traps in the garage. Gabe, their mother's boyfriend, carried the box outside to join the garbage waiting on the curb for collection. Katie wanted to look through the ornaments, but her mother wouldn't let her. "We'll get some new ones, okay?" she said. "We don't want those rat-chewed ones." That night, in bed, Katie dreamt of rats chewing holes in the

Snoopy ornament her father had bought her when they went to Knotts Berry Farm as a family. Scotty got a Charlie Brown ornament, and their mother got Lucy. Try as she might, Katie couldn't remember what ornament their father had bought for himself. The next morning, before school, she ran out to the curb in her bare feet, but the garbage truck had already come and left. The box was gone, as if it had never been there.

In the living room, their father admired the tree. "I did the tinsel," Scotty said, and their father said, "I think it's the best tinseled tree I've ever seen." He turned and asked Katie if she helped with the tinsel, too. "A little," Katie said, even though that was a lie. She had claimed a stomachache and retreated up to her room while her mother and Gabe and Scotty decorated the tree with the new ornaments. Her father smiled at her, and she looked down at her feet, thinking of her cast-away Snoopy, wondering if her father knew what had happened to all the mismatched ornaments they had collected as a family.

Since the divorce, Katie didn't think of her father as part of their family anymore, at least not part of the family that included her mother. It was like she had two families that were planets orbiting in entirely separate atmospheres: she, Scotty and their mother, and sometimes Gabe, in this house she had lived in ever since she could remember; and she, Scotty, and their father, in slices of weekend afternoon time, driving around to fast food restaurants and bowling alleys and mini-golf courses, what her father called "Fun-with-a-capital-F" places that caused Katie's throat to tighten with every minute slipping away, because when afternoon melted into evening and the streetlights blinked on it would be time for their father to take them home and then drive away. He used to take them to the same fast food restaurants and bowling alleys and mini-golf courses and then drive home and stay, because it used to be his home, too. Last Christmas, it had been his home, too.

Their mother came down the stairs, her hair damp from the shower. "Oh," she said when she saw their father. "You're early." She didn't look angry, just surprised.

"I hit all the green lights," their father said. He opened his mouth as if to say something more, but didn't.

Katie hugged her mother goodbye and her chin came up to her mother's shoulder. Her mother had always seemed taller. "You guys be good," she said into Katie's hair.

Their father smiled tightly, the same smile he used to put on when their mother's friends were over. Katie realized their father didn't usually come inside the house. Usually he stood on the front stoop, his hands clasped behind his back, rocking from his heels to his toes, while their mother got Katie and Scotty into jackets and waved goodbye from the doorway, the screen door making her a blurry outline if Katie turned and looked back from the car window as they drove away.

"Dad wanted to see the tree!" Scotty exclaimed. He was still holding their father's hand and he swung it forward and back.

"It's a great tree," their father said, looking down at Scotty. "Did you pick it out yourself, bud?"

"No," Scotty said. The silence stretched. Their mother broke away from Katie and fluffed her damp hair with her hands. After the divorce, she had cut her hair boy-short; now she was growing it out again. She used a straightening iron to flatten it every morning before going to the realty office where she worked as a receptionist. She wouldn't let Katie use a straightening iron on her hair; she was too young, her mother said. Too young for make-up either. People told Katie she had inherited her mother's looks, but now Katie's hair was curly and her mother's hair was unsettlingly straight.

"Gabe brought the tree for you, huh kids?" she said, and Katie hated her. "We've just been so busy. We didn't have time to go pick out one together."

Later that night, Katie will tell her mother that her hair looks ugly. Straightened, the texture is different – thin and stringy, like paintbrush bristles. Nobody could think it looks good, that paintbrush-bristle hair, Katie will say. Except maybe Gabe, who is stupid and ugly, too.

"How's Gabe?" their father asked, glancing at the stairs as if expecting him to appear on the landing, trailing their mother around like a droopy-eyed golden retriever.

"He's fine. He's working today. Putting in extra hours at the office."

"Good, that's good." Their father cleared his throat.

"He got the Christmas tree at Big Wave Dave's," Scotty announced, as if it were something to be proud of. Big Wave Dave's was the only Christmas tree lot in town, materializing the day after Thanksgiving in the otherwise empty square of land where Cartright's used to be. The bus route took Katie past it every day on the way to and from the middle school. Katie and Scotty had begged their mother to take them to pick out a tree, but she was busy stirring pots in the kitchen and talking on the phone to Aunt Carol and resting quietly in the dark of her bedroom ("Just let me be for a little bit, okay?" she'd say. "Go do your homework. We'll get a tree tomorrow.") They didn't get a Christmas tree until Gabe came home lugging one under his arm, its branches uneven, dripping pine needles all over the carpet. Scotty had been immediately overcome with excitement, dancing around the room and throwing tinsel up into the air so it rained down upon the furniture and the braided rug and their sleeping dog, Joey, who was older than both Katie and Scotty and didn't even seem to notice the clumps of silver growing all over his body.

Watching Gabe heft the tree's bulk into the red-and-green Christmas tree stand her mother had filled carefully with water from the kitchen sink, Katie had felt a strange disappointment. Because the Christmas tree itself wasn't the point. The point was going to Big Wave Dave's together, and walking together along the uneven rows between the trees, the air smelling of winter even though it was sixty degrees and sunny outside. The point was inspecting branches for insects and gauging heights for what would be closest to grazing the ceiling of their living room while still leaving room for the angel on top, the angel Katie had saved up her allowance money to buy last Christmas (though it didn't keep her parents from fighting, her mother physically pushing her father out the front door, his shoes only half-on, his head banging against the doorframe – *Ow*, Katie had thought, watching it from the stair landing – but her father hadn't grimaced, hadn't said a word, just walked out the door as her mother yelled and yelled about some woman Noreen, a name Katie didn't recognize.)

Their father bent down and rubbed Joey's ears. "Big Wave Dave's," he said, addressing the dog. "That's fun."

"Fun for Gabe maybe," Katie said.

"Katie, please," her mother said. "Not now."

"What? I'm just saying, picking out the tree is the fun part. Right, Dad?"

Her father scratched Joey under the chin. "I'm sure your mother was just trying to give you a surprise," he said, not looking at her. Katie felt the excitement in her belly flicker and die out. Didn't her father realize she was on his side?

"Whatever," Katie said. She thought her father would understand that the Christmas tree itself wasn't the point. The point was choosing favorites and arguing over them, circling back through the rows of trees, looking and relooking, until finally deciding together on *their* Christmas tree.

"Da-ad," Scotty whined. "Where are we going?"

"It's a surprise," their father said. He met Katie's eyes and winked, an apology. Katie focused her attention on lacing up her tennis shoes.

"Well, you guys have fun," their mother said. She looked small and alone, standing there on the stairs with her damp hair.

"I'll have them back by six," their father said.

Their mother walked them to the doorway, but she didn't wave goodbye through the screen. When Katie looked back, the front door was closed, like the hard shell of a turtle protecting itself. Through the living room window, the Christmas tree blinked on and off, on and off.

"Where are we going?" Scotty asked.

"It's a surprise," their father said. No matter how many times Scotty asked, that was all their father would say in response. He drove them through town, past the mini-golf course and bowling alley and laser tag, past the McDonald's and Wendy's and Burger King. A red light stopped them beside Big Wave Dave's. Katie looked out the car window at the blur of tree branches and thought about Cartright's, remembered how they all used to go there together, she and Scotty and their father and mother, back before it burned down. Cartright's had been a taco restaurant painted bright yellow with yellow booths made of hard plastic. They served the tacos in wire baskets shaped like boats and they made their own corn tortillas in the kitchen. One time, Mr. Reynosa let Katie and Scotty go back to the kitchen and try a tortilla fresh from the stovetop. Mr. Reynosa wore an apron with the Mexican flag stitched across the front and he kept small brightly wrapped candies in a bowl by the register. As their mother threw away used napkins and their father counted out bills from his wallet, Mr. Reynosa would ask Katie and Scotty, "Are you being good kids?"

"Yes," they would say, solemn-voiced.

"Have a candy." Mr. Reynosa's eyes would squint into the folds of his smile-wrinkles, and Katie and Scotty would carefully pluck candies from the bowl, one piece each, which they would savor slowly (Katie) or chomp to bits (Scotty) on the drive home, the windows down, their father whistling along to the radio, their mother tapping her fingers to the beat.

But that was a long time ago – two, maybe even three years had passed since the building burned down. Looking out the car window, Katie tried to remember the details of Cartright's exterior, but her memory of it had grown blurrier the more time passed. Was the parking lot in the front, or the back? Were there bushes planted along the walkway? What color was the sign? She couldn't remember. Just her parents sitting on the same side of the bright yellow booth and the hard smoothness of the candy against her tongue, before it melted away to nothing.

"Dad, where are we going?" Scotty asked again.

"It's a surprise," their father said. He didn't look at them in the rear-view mirror the way he usually did. The light turned green and they drove on, through the rest of town, onto the freeway heading north. This was the section of the freeway Katie loved most – the ocean on one side, the mountains on the other. The ocean was on Scotty's side of the car. Katie looked out her window at the mountains, their grassy coats a tentative green instead of the usual brown. It had rained a good amount since Thanksgiving, enough to keep the wildfires at bay, and Katie was happy because rain meant colder weather and colder weather meant it felt more like winter, more like Christmas.

They drove for what felt like a long time, past the beach house shaped like a castle, past the little town that had been half-buried by a landslide a few years before, past the exits for Santa Barbara, where their parents used to live before she was born. Katie had been there a handful of times on field trips to the zoo or the art museum. To her, Santa Barbara seemed pretty much the same as the town they lived in, but her mother acted like it was worlds away. "Now *that*," her mother would say, "is a nice town. Classy people. Best place I ever lived."

"Why'd you move, then?" Katie asked once.

Her mother was folding laundry on the couch. "Things happen," she said. "Life happens." She looked down at one of Scotty's shirts, folding it carefully in half, like a mirror image pressed against itself.

"Seems pretty dumb to move away," Katie said. It was a Saturday evening, after her father had dropped them off and waved goodbye, and she was feeling mean and pent-up and broken. She pressed on, wanting her mother to look up, wanting to see hurt in her eyes. "I mean, if you loved it so much. It sounds like you didn't love it enough."

"Yes I did," her mother said in a soft voice. "I loved it there." Years from now, Katie will learn that her parents had moved out of Santa Barbara because her father lost his job, and her mother couldn't afford to continue attending classes at the City College, which was the whole reason she had moved there in the first place. Katie had not known her mother ever attended college. She didn't know her parents' settling down had been, for her mother, a form of settling, the kind of happiness that leaves a bitter aftertaste.

Past Santa Barbara, on the outskirts of Goleta, their father flicked on the turn signal and they eased off the freeway onto a residential street edged with palm trees.

"Where are we going?" Scotty asked, bouncing in his seat. "Are we almost there?"

"Soon." Their father glanced at the map printed out from the computer, directions angled towards him on the passenger seat. Katie watched the palm trees bob their heads in the breeze.

Their car pulled up to a large park, soccer and baseball fields stretching as far as Katie could see. They drove through the open yellow gate, along a well-speedbumped road – Scotty bouncing gleefully in his seat with each bump – past a community swimming pool and tennis courts. The next parking lot they came to was marked with a big arrow and a cardboard sign: SNOW WORLD PARKING HERE.

"Snow World?" Katie asked. "Is that where we're going?"

"Snow World?" Scotty said. "What's Snow World?"

Their father pulled the car into a spot and cut the engine. He turned around, his smile proud. "I told you I'd take you to the snow, didn't I?"

33

And it was true, he had told them so – earlier that year, in late spring. Scotty had gotten into trouble at school for leading a group of fellow second-graders in jumping off the jungle gym, working up higher and higher until a teacher stopped them. Their mother told Scotty not to play that game anymore, that he could get hurt, but Scotty was stubborn. Over soda and pizza at the bowling alley, their father told them about the time he broke his leg when he was a boy in a small town in Ohio, sledding with his brothers down McArthur's Hill. Their father didn't talk about his brothers often, so when he did, Katie and Scotty paid attention.

"Let me tell you, son," their father said to Scotty, leaning close over the soda-sticky table. "Breaking your leg hurts!"

Scotty nodded, biting his straw.

"No more jumping off the jungle gym. Okay? And stop chewing on that straw."

"Dad," Scotty said. "What's snow like?"

"Snow? Well, it's fun to play in. You can go sledding. Have snowball fights. Build snowmen."

"Like in the Christmas movies?"

Their father laughed. "Just like in the Christmas movies. We'll go to the snow sometime. How's that sound?"

"Yeah!" said Scotty, and Katie nodded, smiling fully, forgetting that she didn't like the crookedness of her front teeth so she only smiled with her lips closed. That night, she dreamt of making snow angels on the front lawn. The dream-snow felt like feathers brushing against her back and shoulders.

Katie and Scotty climbed out of the car. The sun was hot on the tops of their heads, and heat rose up from the black pavement of the parking lot. Scotty wriggled out of his jacket, but their father insisted on bringing it with them. "You'll want this," he said. "I don't want you to get cold playing in the snow all afternoon." Katie kept her jacket on and, as they walked towards the park, she could feel sweat gathering on her skin, dampening her T-shirt. *Snow*, she thought, unable to curb the rising excitement inside her. *Real snow.*

They followed the arrows to a giant banner reading SNOW WORLD that was strung between two trees. At the entrance a folding table was set up, where an old lady wearing a puff-painted Rudolph shirt took their father's money and handed them three construction-paper tickets taped to mini candy-canes. "Have fun!" she said, waving at them, the bells on her sweatshirt jingling softly. Scotty tugged on their father's hand, leading them under the banner, into an area of the park marked off by plastic fencing. Icicle lights were strung along tree branches, the tiny bulbs dull-looking in the brightness of the sun. Christmas music blared from loudspeakers.

Katie did not see any snow. Just grass, dirt, trees – just a regular park, decorated with Christmas lights and cut-outs of Santa Claus and elves and reindeer. Giant candy-canes sprung from the grass like strange flowers. Groups of kids ran by in T-shirts and shorts. Moms carried babies and held hands of toddlers. Most of the kids there looked Scotty's age or younger. There were no older kids like her, and no teenagers either, except for a few high-schoolers working the Sno-Cone stand and the hot chocolate booth. Katie wished she could roll back time and make herself younger, smaller. The older she got, the more unwieldy and wrong her life felt. It scared her – the way she could only go forward, never back.

I'm moving forward, Katie had heard her mother say on the phone to Aunt Carol shortly after the divorce was finalized. Sometimes, Katie would cut class and walk home, slipping into her own backyard without her mother knowing. She would sit on the grass, back pressed against the wall underneath the kitchen window, and braid dandelion stems together. When the window was open, she could hear her mother talking. *He made his own bed. And you know what they say – it's a symptom of a larger problem. We'd been having problems for a while.* The next week, for Valentine's Day, their mother went on a double-date with a woman from work, and that's how she met Gabe.

"C'mon, Katie!" Scotty called. He was a few feet ahead, dragging their father towards a hill at the far end of the park. "Sledding!"

Katie followed, glancing into an area marked "Snow Play Zone" as they walked past. The ground was muddy, the grass stomped flat by the zigzag footsteps of running children – yet there, in the middle of it all, was a knee-high lump of snow, gleaming. She wanted to run over and press her fingers into it. She wanted to feel snow melting under her fingernails. And then she wanted to step on it, crush it – feel all the snow turning to mud under her tennis shoes.

At the bottom of the sledding hill, Katie joined her father (frowning) and Scotty (bouncing). "Hmm," their father murmured. "There was supposed to be snow." It looked like there had been snow at one time, but most of it had melted. Kids caromed down the hill, their sleds leaving trails of mud in the grass and slush. The sleds were bright green and made of a flimsy plastic that reminded Katie of her school binder. Scotty held his in one hand and waved his arm up and down so the plastic wiggled. "Cool!" he said. "Dad, look!"

"That's neat, bud," their father said. His face looked caved in.

Their father had moved most of his things out of their house while Katie and Scotty were at school. He'd left a note propped on Katie's dresser, a folded piece of paper that said, simply, *I love you. I'll see you soon.* Her name was on the front – *K8*, her father's shorthand, her lucky number. When he lived with them, he had given her eight quarters for her allowance every week. Her chores had been helping her father with his weekend tasks – mowing the lawn, trimming the bushes, washing her mother's car. Her father drove a mud-splattered Jeep that they never washed. He told her the guys would make fun of him if he drove up to the construction site on Monday with no dirt on his Jeep.

Now, her father stared up at the muddy hill, his eyes squinting in the sun. Katie picked up her green plastic sled from the soggy grass.

"It looks fun, Dad," Katie said. "It's still sledding. It counts." She took Scotty's hand and they trudged together up the hill. Their father stood at the bottom, watching them. When they got to the top, they waved. Their father seemed far away. He waved back, still holding Scotty's jacket in the other arm.

"Ready?" Katie asked.

"Yeah," Scotty said.

Later – after they built a small lopsided snowman and ate Sno-Cones and returned to the big hill, where Scotty purposefully veered his sled into a tree and sprained his wrist; after Katie entered middle school and began grazing a razor blade against her thighs; after their mother married Gabe and withdrew even further into herself; after their father died on a clear-skied February morning, when his Jeep slammed into a Lexus that had careened over the center divider – later, when Katie would think back on Snow World, she would think about that moment when she and Scotty first sat down on their bright green plastic sleds at the top of that hill, looked at each other, took a deep breath, and pushed off, sliding down in the slush and the mud, faster and faster, more thrilling than any roller coaster. She'd remember her breathlessness and the pure glee in Scotty's shrieks. How they both skidded to a stop at the bottom, and without a word picked up their plastic sleds and raced to the top – eager to capture the magic again, and again, the thrill of barreling down the hill towards their father and knowing he would be there, squinting in the sun, waiting for them.

Erik and Steffy

Erik's sister Steffy appears late at night and pesters him. He never knew her in life because she died before he was born. Steffy says it doesn't matter, they're linked by blood. Erik ages day by month by year, but Steffy remains seven years old.

She loves old people activities: crossword puzzles, chess, knitting. Apparently there are a lot of old people where she is now. She likes collecting facts and then fanning them out before Erik like a deck of playing cards on a green felt table.

She begins each fact with, "Did you know?" She tries to impress him.

When Erik was younger, he believed everything Steffy said. Nightfall found him a jumble of excitement, wondering if his sister would come. He'd sit patiently through the bedtime stories his parents read him, close his eyes and pretend to drift off to sleep, feeling relief at his mother's cool kiss on his forehead or his father's gentle head pat, the murmur of their footfalls on his carpet, the squeak of his bedroom door closing. When Erik opened his eyes, the only light in the room would be a small sliver of yellow creeping under his bedroom door from the hallway. His best friend from school, Scott, liked his bedroom door left slightly ajar, and when Erik slept over at Scott's house, he had gradually grown accustomed to falling asleep with light seeping into the room. But Erik preferred darkness. In the lamplight, Steffy was slightly translucent, hazy, as if she could fade away at any moment. In the darkness, she seemed realer somehow. Like a real sister. After Erik's mother or father gently shut his bedroom door, he would whisper, "Steffy? Steffy?" feeling a buzzing tightness in his chest, his eagerness to see her coupled with fear that she would not come. At the sight of her gap-toothed smile, her eyes exactly the same shade of green as his own, Erik would feel an overwhelming sense of wholeness – as if he were being reunited with an older, wiser piece of his own self.

But that was a long time ago. Now, Erik is a junior in high school. His moments of connection with his sister are few and far between; when she visits, he feels like he is babysitting. He is overwhelmed by all the things Steffy doesn't know, all the things he can't talk to her about because she wouldn't understand. Like his frustration with Scott, who keeps cutting class to drive around town and smoke joints under the pier. Erik went with him once, but it was boring and the joint made him sick and he doesn't want to do it again. Still, Scott keeps asking. Which isn't the problem, not really – what Erik really worries about is the day Scott stops asking, because it will mean he has new friends and doesn't need Erik anymore. Erik can't help but remember the sleepover in sixth grade when they pricked their fingers and became blood brothers and swore to be best friends forever. Steffy wouldn't understand friendships past second grade; how they become complicated.

And she certainly wouldn't understand his ever-present desire for Emily Harrow, who sits behind him in Physics and who he danced with at Diana Wheeler's party two months ago. Emily hadn't seemed drunk but maybe she had been, maybe she doesn't remember dancing with him at all, because she doesn't talk to him other than occasionally asking what answer he got for a homework problem. Erik tried telling Steffy about Emily, one night a few weeks ago when he was feeling particularly alone. Steffy said Erik should make Emily a bracelet or give her some of the cookies from his lunch. And Erik felt even more alone and pathetic and weird – here he was, trying to get dating advice from the ghost of his seven-year-old sister. Now, more than anything, Steffy's visits remind him that he is different from everyone else. Erik wonders if that's why even normal things like dancing with a girl at a party or cutting class with your best friend seem, for him, to be minefields of difficulty.

"Did you know," Steffy says now, "that dolphins never ever sleep?"

"What do you mean, they never sleep?" Erik says. "That's impossible."

"It's true!" Steffy insists. Her auburn hair, braided in pigtails, shimmers in the lamplight. Erik's desk lamp is the only light in the room. He is working on a six-to-eight-page paper about the role of the supernatural in *Hamlet*. The paper is due first period, so he can't skip his first few classes to finish it.

Steffy is perched on the edge of Erik's desk, swinging her legs so her heels thump an uneven rhythm against the wooden drawers where Erik keeps his old notebooks and school papers and the shoebox of Steffy's things.

"Hey," Erik says. "Stop that."

"What?"

"Stop kicking your legs like that."

"Why?"

"Cause it's annoying."

"Why?"

"Cause I'm trying to write this paper."

"Why?"

"Cause it's due in seven hours and I'm trying to *concentrate*, okay?" Erik cracks his neck and leans further forward, zeroing in on the soft blue glow of his laptop screen.

Steffy stops swinging her legs. She pulls a cherry lollypop from the front pocket of her jumper and takes an especially long time opening it. The wrapper crinkles loudly in the dim, still room. Erik's hands are poised on the keyboard, but his fingers don't move.

"Erik," Steffy says after a few moments. "*Eriiiik.*"

"What?"

"It's true. Dolphins never sleep. It's *true!*"

"Uh-huh," Erik murmurs, eyes focused on the computer screen. This infuriates Steffy more than anything — blank, patronizing agreement. She lapses back into silence.

The white stick of her lollypop shifts between her teeth. He can sense her thinking.

"But Erik," she says. "Then why did you say it was impossible?"

"Huh?"

"*I* said that dolphins never ever sleep and *you* said that was impossible. Why?"

"Because."

"Because why?"

"Cause every living being needs to sleep." As soon as the words leave his mouth Erik feels a flare of regret, worried he's offended her. But Steffy, fixated on the dolphins, seems undisturbed.

It's been twenty-one years since she died, four years before he was born, Erik calculates. Perhaps she doesn't remember what sleeping is like.

"But *Eriiiiik.*" Steffy pulls the lollypop from her mouth and points it at him. "There's a way they *do* it."

"What?"

"Go without sleep. Dolphins. What they do is, their brains – part of their brain is awake, and part of their brain is sleeping. Then the awake part goes to sleep and the sleeping part wakes up. So they *are* always awake. Get it?"

"Where'd you learn that?"

"From Miss Y." Steffy smiles triumphantly. Her teeth are stained pink from the lollypop and her right front tooth is missing. She lost it two days before she died, biting into a carrot at dinner. The tooth fairy brought her fifty cents. She was outraged to learn, when Erik's baby teeth began falling out, that the tooth fairy brought him a full dollar. He had offered to split the money with her, but she had laughed and said, "Oh, we don't use money." Still, Erik remembers how she glanced wistfully at his stacks of quarters lined up like toy soldiers on the bookcase beside his bed. Once he caught her trying to pocket a few. She could pick them up all right, hold them in the palm of her hand like a real person could, but when she tried to drop them into her jumper pocket they fell straight through onto Erik's linty carpet floor.

This happened with everything Erik tried to give her: dried butterflies, a friendship bracelet, a picture he drew for her of a dog inside a doghouse. Steffy can hold things and play with things while she is with him, but she can take nothing with her when she departs. The only item that travels with her is the cherry lollypop in her jumper pocket, the lollypop she put there the day she died and now enjoys eternally. As a kid, Erik kept his older sister's things atop his nightstand in neatly arranged rows, ready and waiting for her next visit. Now her things languish in a shoebox in his bottom desk drawer. Recently, more than once, he has almost thrown the whole shoebox out. But he can never go through with it.

Many times throughout the years Erik has asked Steffy about Heaven, but she remains vague and noncommittal. She won't even call it Heaven – she just says, "Where I live." She seems content there. She doesn't seem to miss her life or their parents much, though she does talk often about her second-grade teacher, Miss Y., who Erik can tell she adored. Most of her "Did you knows" are things she supposedly learned from Miss Y. Erik remembers how excited he had been for second grade. The way Steffy talked about it, he thought every second-grader had Miss Y. for a teacher, the same way "b" always came after "a" in the alphabet and they always said the Pledge of Allegiance first thing at school assemblies. When his teacher was instead a doughy-faced, grandmotherly Mrs. Peckbody, Erik had come home in tears, so acute was his disappointment.

Later, he learned that Miss Y. had stopped teaching and moved to Montana. She had probably gotten married by now, expunging the Miss Y. and replacing it with something else.

Sometimes he tries to imagine what it must have been like, the day of Steffy's accident. Not for Steffy, or even for his parents – Steffy and his parents are too real to him – but what it must have been like for Miss Y., the mythical shadow he half-knows from Steffy's stream of stories. The older Erik gets, the more pain he feels for his sister's second-grade teacher. Poor Miss Y. Her first year teaching. Steffy slips and falls on the tetherball courts during morning recess, whacking her head on the unforgiving blacktop. She cries, of course, and is ushered to the Nurse's Office for a Band-Aid and an icepack and a cherry lollypop. She seems fine, and within ten minutes she's back at her desk in Room 17, giggling with her seat partner Rosie about the class pet, Tom the Tortoise, who sometimes eats his own poop. But then during math drills Steffy starts acting loopy and confused, like a seven-year-old who's downed a glass of wine, and then an hour later she's in a coma, and then two days later she's dead. No wonder Miss Y. quit teaching and moved thousands of miles away.

The first day of second grade, the day Erik came home crying about Mrs. Peckbody, was the first and last time he told his parents about Steffy's visits. His mother was alarmed at his "fixation" on his dead sister and convinced his father that they should take Erik to see Dr. Lassen, a child psychologist. Dr. Lassen wasn't recommended to them; Erik's mother met him at a Starbucks when their orders were accidentally switched. Looking back, Erik now suspects they had an affair, because his parents' marriage disintegrated soon after. Dr. Lassen wore knit caps and hemp flip-flops. He would give Erik a 64-box of crayons and a stack of blank paper and then disappear for twenty or thirty minutes, likely into his back office with Erik's mother. And then he would reappear, crouching down to look at what Erik had drawn, murmuring a lot of "Uhhms" and "Ahhhs" and occasionally sighing quick bursts of breath out of his nostrils like a horse.

Dr. Lassen's office was in an old converted fitness center and you could still see hooks on the ceiling where the rock-climbing wall had been anchored. Erik went to see him every Wednesday for three months, during the course of which they never talked about Steffy or school or his parents.

Dr. Lassen never said much of anything, really, other than his murmuring and snorting.

One night, Steffy asked Erik about Dr. Lassen. "What do you do during your visits?" she said, flopping down beside Erik on his bottom bunk.

"He gives me crayons and I draw things," Erik said.

"What things?"

"Monsters and dragons and things."

"I wanna see!" Steffy sat up, tugging her pigtails in excitement.

"They're in my backpack. I'll show you later." Steffy lay back down, which made Erik feel bad. "Hey Steffy?" he said. "What if next time I draw you a picture?"

"Really?"

"Yeah. What do you want me to draw?"

"A dog," Steffy said. "A dog in a doghouse."

"Okay."

"Make his name be Max. Okay, Erik? Write Max on the doghouse."

"Why Max?"

"Because I used to have a dog named Max."

"You did?"

"Yeah."

"Was he a good dog?"

"Yeah. I'd throw tennis balls and he'd race after them and then he'd run back and drop them at my feet."

"He would?"

"Yeah. And you know the avocado tree in the backyard? Sometimes I'd pick avocados and throw them for Max to fetch – you know, trying to trick him. But he wouldn't fetch avocados. He knew the difference. He was really smart."

"Do you miss him?"

Steffy nodded. She smoothed the blanket with her hands and didn't meet Erik's eyes.

In March, abruptly, Erik's visits to Dr. Lassen stopped, and the framed school portraits of Steffy on the mantel and in the hallway came down, as did the macaroni magnet she had painted and glued in the early days of Miss Y.'s class that still hung on the fridge. Erik's parents told him that Steffy was gone forever, and no good would come from talking about her because it would be best for all of them to move on, and they wanted Erik to know that they loved him very, very much and he didn't have to worry about competing with Steffy, it wasn't like that; they missed Steffy, of course, but they loved him so very, very much, and what happened to Steffy was an accident and Erik was a healthy, strong, smart little boy and he didn't need to worry, he would live to be an old, old man, yes, old like his Grandpa Joe, and they just loved him so very, very much, did he know how much they loved him?

Two months later, his parents divorced. His dad moved into an apartment the next town over that smelled like eggs. He came to visit Erik every other weekend, taking him to the zoo and Chuck E. Cheese and the big park with the swirly slide, but afterwards he would drive Erik home and get back into his car by himself and drive away, and every time Erik cried and had trouble falling asleep. Steffy began to visit more often. Erik would pull the blankets up to his chin and roll over and there his sister would be: perching on his windowsill; dancing the Ooba Jooba on his desk; hanging upside-down from the slats of his bunk bed, her hair a shiny curtain, making monkey faces at him until he laughed. Sometimes she did cartwheels across his floor, from one wall of his room to the other. Other times she curled beside him in bed and stroked his hair until sleep finally came. Her fingers didn't feel like real fingers, but rather like a soothing, gentle breeze, the kind of breeze that doesn't exist in real life, only in dreams. Erik would fall asleep to her facts:

"Did you know that all of the tallest mountains in the world are in Asia?"

"Did you know that every time you sneeze some of your brain cells die?"

"Did you know that Dalmatians are born without spots?"

"Dalmatians!" Erik exclaimed. "I want a Dalmatian. Mom and Dad won't let me get a dog." He sighed and marched his fingers along the wooden slats of the bunk bed above them. "Mom and Dad don't believe me."

"Don't believe what?" Steffy asked.

"They don't believe you come see me."

"*Eriiiiik.*" He turned his head on the pillow and looked at her. The whites of her eyes seemed huge in the dark. "You told them?" Steffy asked quietly.

Erik felt his neck and face flush. "Yeah."

"Oh, no." Steffy shook her head in a way that made Erik's stomach curdle anxiously. "Erik, you can't do that. Don't mention our visits to them again."

"It was just one time."

"You can't tell *anyone* about our visits."

"Not even Scotty?"

"No."

"Why not?" Erik asked.

"Because no one else would believe you. They'd all think you're crazy."

"Why?"

"Because some things only brothers and sisters understand. Okay?"

Erik sighed. "Okay."

"Promise?"

"I promise," Erik said. He was surprised Steffy didn't visit their mother and father. Steffy sighed and said she had tried once, a long time ago, but their mother started wailing and their father acted like he didn't see her. Erik told Steffy their father lived in an apartment now, a smelly apartment far away.

"How far away?" Steffy asked.

"All the way past Big Wave Dave's, on the other side of the river."

Steffy didn't say anything, just stroked Erik's hair and blew a single breeze-kiss on his cheek.

But that was a long time ago. Erik doesn't need Steffy's facts or goodnight kisses anymore. He has no trouble falling asleep. It's his damn schoolwork that's the trouble, keeping him up so late. Given the choice, Erik would have fled to dreamland hours ago.

"Erik?" Steffy says. "Did you know – "

"Stef, seriously," Erik interrupts. "No more. Okay? I'm busy." He leans closer to his computer screen, trying to refocus his attention.

Steffy bites into her lollypop, loudly crunching the shards of red candy between her teeth. For a few minutes, the room is quiet save for the sounds of crunching and typing. Then –

"Did you know this is my last visit?" Steffy says quietly.

Erik looks over at her. "What?"

"This is my last visit." She tosses the pink-tipped lollypop stick towards his trash can; it ricochets off the lip and lands on the carpet a couple feet away.

Erik feels a strange panic rise in his throat. He swallows. "What do you mean, your last visit?"

Steffy shrugs. "I'm not coming back anymore after this."

"Why not?"

"I have to go somewhere else."

"Somewhere else? Where?"

Steffy shrugs again. "I have to leave pretty soon. I just wanted to say goodbye."

"Goodbye? What the hell?" Erik pushes his chair away from his desk, surprised at the sudden alarm pounding in his chest. "Steffy, you can't just disappear on me forever."

"Sorry. I have to."

"I mean, there's still – don't you have more facts or something to tell me?"

47

Ever since the latter half of middle school, when Erik began to realize that the other, normal kids in his grade didn't still have invisible friends – much less invisible friends who weren't really invisible or make-believe but rather spirits of their dead siblings – he has often been short to Steffy, feeling vaguely embarrassed and easily annoyed by her incessant questions and farfetched stories and elementary-school lingo.

Still, Erik always figured that if Steffy stopped visiting, it would be because *he* initiated it – because he told her he needed space, or because he moved away and moved on with his life and had no more time for childish games and "Did you knows." Even then, Erik always assumed he would still see Steffy occasionally – maybe she would drop by on his birthday every year, or she would visit when he came home for Christmas. They would be like normal grown-up siblings, like their mother and her sisters, who live on opposite coasts but still talk to each other on the phone, laughing about old relatives and old memories that nobody else understands in quite the same way.

Erik rises from his chair and goes to her. He stands in front of his desk, stooping slightly so their eyes are level. "Steffy," he says. "You're serious about this? You're not just trying to get my attention?"

She shakes her head.

"You're really never coming back?"

His sister smiles an old lady smile, a crossword puzzles and knitting smile. "Never ever," she says.

Erik sighs. "Why not?"

Steffy doesn't say anything, just reaches out and touches his hair like she used to.

"Man," Erik says. "I didn't know our time was…was limited like this."

Looking at his sister, Erik is overwhelmed by a frustrating helplessness. Why did she have to fall on the playground that day? What if she had landed differently, fallen forward instead of backward? What if she were a real person, a real sister, and he could be annoyed and angry and short with her and not have to worry about her fading away to nothingness and never coming back?

"I didn't tell anyone," Erik says. "If that's why."

"No – "

"Except for that one slip to Mom and Dad. I never told anyone else about your visits."

"I know, Erik," Steffy says. "You're a good brother." She hops down from her perch on his desk and hugs him around the waist. The top of her head comes up to his chest. "I'll miss you," she says, breaking away and smiling up at him. She is waning by the moment, growing translucent around the edges.

"Hey, Steffy, wait!" Erik bends down, opens the bottom drawer of his desk, and pulls out the faded Nike shoebox from four shoe sizes ago. "Don't forget your stuff."

"I can't take it with me."

"Even this last time?"

"I don't think so."

"Just try," Erik insists. He picks up the braided friendship bracelet he made for her at summer camp when he was nine and gently ties it around her wrist.

"Thanks," Steffy says.

"You're welcome."

"Hey Erik?"

"What?"

"Did you know that you're my frother?"

"What's a frother?" he asks.

"A friend plus a brother. A frother. Get it?"

"Yeah," Erik says. "That's a good one." Before he can say more, that he loves her and he's sorry for all the times he snapped at her and she's his frother, too – no, wait, his *frister*, she's his frister – Steffy is gone. The friendship bracelet thumps softly onto the carpet.

Erik picks it up and places it back in the shoebox, tears stinging his eyes. He closes the shoebox and sets it back in the bottom drawer. Then he turns out the desk light, curls into bed, and falls asleep. He dreams of running beside the ocean, the salty breeze cool and soft against his face.

Erik gets a B-minus on his *Hamlet* essay. Later that week, he strikes up a conversation with Emily Harrow by offering her half of the giant cookie he bought at the school snack bar, and at Diana Wheeler's next party, they kiss. Scott gets busted for marijuana possession and his mom and stepdad send him to a strict boarding school across the country. Erik writes him a letter and, after much deliberation, signs it, "Your blood brother." Scott writes back and invites Erik to visit him in Ann Arbor, which Erik does, and things feel different between them yet also the same, and on the last night of Erik's visit they get drunk and prick their fingers again, blood brothers renewed. Senior year, Erik's father remarries and moves out of the egg-smelling apartment and into a new housing tract where Big Wave Dave's used to be.

When Erik leaves for college, his mother converts his bedroom into a home gym. She finds an old shoebox in his bottom desk drawer filled with melted candy, brittle pine cones and dried-up bugs. There is one drawing, of a dog inside a doghouse, "MAX" scrawled across the top in Erik's child handwriting, that gives her pause. How would Erik have known about Max? She guesses they must have mentioned him at some point, just as they had mentioned Steffy. It's funny, what kids latch on to. She closes her eyes, seeing Steffy's pudgy toddler legs, her auburn curls, throwing avocados off the tree in their backyard for Max to fetch.

Erik's mother shakes her head to clear the memory. She smoothes the drawing flat on Erik's desk, thinking she'll keep it here for him to see when he comes home for Thanksgiving. Or maybe she'll mail it to him at school. No, it might embarrass him. He's not her little boy anymore. *No matter what*, she thinks, *our children always leave us.* She keeps the drawing but tosses the rest of the shoebox into the trash, feeling strangely out of sorts.

She picks up the phone and dials. "Hi, Alice," she says. "I was just thinking about that time Mom made us get those awful Page-boy haircuts, remember?" Alice brings up the Matching Dress Fiasco of 1963, and before long they're both laughing the loud nasally laugh they inherited from their father, the genuine unharnessed laugh that only emerges around each other.

Hanging up half an hour later, Erik's mother thinks again of Steffy and wishes, for the millionth time, that her son could have known his sister.

Slowly, Slowly, Without Much Notice

3642 Maplewood Drive is a three-story flagstone house with a gabled roof and four-car garage, nestled deep within the protective arms of Red Fern Ranch, which is not a ranch at all but rather a gated community in a southern California suburb not much nuisanced by crime to begin with. In this neighborhood, the houses preen. Windows sparkle. The sidewalks are dutifully swept; the curbs are free of debris; parked cars do not clutter the streets. If one's lawn ventures into unkempt neglect, the Homeowner's Association sends a firm-but-gentle reminder by way of a firm-but-gentle fine. At 3642 Maplewood Drive, gardeners come every Wednesday morning to trim the hedges, mow the lawn, rake the leaves.

A family lives here. A father, a mother, and a son. The Sampsons.

I am born at 3642 Maplewood Drive at 8:53 pm on a Friday night. Not a soul in Red Fern Ranch knows about me. It is a dry, still night, static electricity palpable in the air. I am born in the attic.

On this Friday night, minutes after my birth, an argument simmers in the ornately tiled kitchen. The son – Jared, a high school senior, admitted to Berkeley next fall – wants to go out with his friends. But his mother is adamantly against him going anywhere.

"I just have a feeling," she says. "A bad feeling. I can't explain it."

Jared looks down at the granite countertop, silently runs his finger along the grout between the tiles.

"Please, honey. Stay here tonight, will you? Safe and sound."

"I'll be safe, Mom. I promise."

"Honey – "

"I won't even be out that late."

The father stamps into the kitchen and bangs cabinets, opening and closing them at random. He settles upon a bag of trail mix, which he pours into his palm. "Listen to your mother," he says, using his no-arguing voice.

"I promise I won't be out late."

"Jared, what have we talked about?"

The son sighs. "Fine. I'll be a loser with no social life."

The mother's face relaxes. She had felt tears welling up inside her, but she was able to tamp them down before an outburst overtook all thought. She smiles gratefully at George, reaches over and strokes Jared's hair. For a few moments, he stands there and lets her.

"Thank you," she says – to George, to Jared, to them both.

It is 9:02 p.m.

We cannot choose the circumstances in which we are born. Once I am sparked to life, a single thought drives my existence: consume.

All I know is, I am ravenous. I cannot stop myself.

Jared ducks away from his mother and heads up to his bedroom.

"There's a movie on HBO tonight you might like!" his father calls after him. "Some apocalypse action movie."

No response, other than the clomping of Jared's tennis shoes on the stairs.

George looks at Marie and shrugs. She shrugs in return, giving him a playful smile before turning away, her attention snagged by the sink full of dirty dishes. She is wearing a long skirt that clings to her hips. Her hair, dyed a dark brown, gleams in the warm kitchen light. George is swept by the feeling of how it used to be – the two of them, together, apart from everyone else.

It is this feeling that spurs him across the kitchen, wiping the peanut crumbs off his palms. Marie is bent over the big kitchen sink, arms in sudsy water, rinsing pasta sauce off dinner plates and dressing out of salad bowls. George watches her shadowy reflection in the darkened kitchen window, her eyes cast downward, absorbed in her task. The steamy water fills the sink, a continuous rushing sound. He stands behind her, inching closer, closer, and then he's pressed to her, wrapping his arms around her waist, kissing her soft neck.

She flinches, her body stiffening. George pulls away. She turns the water off and flicks her hands once, twice, three times. When she turns, finally, her expression reminds George of a frightened animal – of the squirrel they found one summer, trapped in the attic, desperate to find a way out.

"I'm sorry," she says. "It's just – I've told you – it's hard for me, right now. Being touched."

George takes another step away from her. He runs his hand over his thinning hair, back, forward, back.

"It's not you," she says. "It's not anything to do with you."

"It feels that way, though."

"It's not, I swear. I love you. I'm just – I'm not there yet."

But will you ever get there? George wants to ask. *Will you ever be my wife again?* Eight months since they've made love. Two months since her last breakdown, when she was put on that new medication.

"It's just that you've seemed better lately," he says. "I thought I could kiss you without... frightening you away."

"It's not you, George."

"I guess I was mistaken. Sorry." He raps his knuckles twice on the countertop. His smile is forced, worse than a frown. "I'll be upstairs in my study," he says. He works as a neurologist at the local hospital. "Got some emails to send."

Marie nods and turns back to the dishes. The water is scalding, but she doesn't turn it colder. She watches her hands, scrubbing the delicate china. She watches them as if

they are someone else's hands. Her skin is a bright pink. *Maybe,* she thinks. *Maybe tonight. Maybe I can try to stand it.*
It is 9:14 p.m.

Once you are alive, it is impossible to know what it was like before life. Yet I can taste memories all around me. This cluttered attic is drowning in memories. Christmas tinsel caught around a popsicle-stick ornament. A Kodak Instamatic with half a roll of unused film inside. A child's rocking chair carved from redwood, a delicacy.

I devour the memories, and then they disappear and I am left famished, raging for more. I am suffocating. I need oxygen. I need to breathe.

Jared flops backwards onto his bed, feeling suffocated in the emptiness of his bedroom, the vast hardwood floors stretching around him like a wasteland. He wants to be in a small room crowded with noise and people. He wants a stranger to spill a drink on his shoes; he wants a girl to sob into his shoulder. He wants to dance in the crushing sweaty heart of an L.A. nightclub. He wants to stumble out onto a darkened street and have no idea where he is what time it is or how he got there. He wants to be reckless, to dare life: *C'mon, send me the best you've got. I'm ready.*

His cell phone buzzes. Jared ignores it, knowing it's Scott or Mark or Bryan, one of the guys wanting to know what time he'll be there tonight. If their parents give them a hard time about going out, they go anyway. Or they sneak out later, or they lie about where they're going. Jared has never been able to lie. His face burns and his words run together. And it's gotten worse since his mother's last episode. She's always been an anxious person, fluttery and hands-wringy, moved to tears by burnt breakfast toast, but Jared never thought he would see her like that. Curled into a ball on the floor of her walk-in closet, her eyes huge and far away. Rocking back and forth, back and forth, in a slow terrifying mechanical way. The doctors later referred to it as a panic attack, and she has been back to normal since then, her medication living calmly in the kitchen cupboard alongside the multivitamins and Tums. But Jared can't shake the image of her, wild-eyed and quivering, and he worries that any little thing could send her reeling back to that dark place. And what if the next time, she doesn't recover? What if her small yellow pills no longer work? What then?

His phone buzzes again. Jared pushes himself off his bed and reaches for it. Bryan.

"So what time you want me to pick you up?"

"I don't know," Jared says. "I don't know if I'm going."

"Dude, don't bail out now. You always bail."

"It's just…you know how strict my parents are."

"So sneak out. It's not a big deal. Listen, I'll pick you up at the corner across from the movie theater."

"I'll try."

"Quit this 'trying' bullshit, just be there at 10. Okay? Your parents will be asleep by then anyway. They'll never know the difference."

"Better make it 10:30," Jared says.

"Sure, 10:30. But seriously, don't bail on me, all right? I'm doing this for you."

"I know." Jared's social standing has nosedived the past few months. He's declined so many invitations that he's fading into anonymity. Bryan, his best friend since sixth grade, confided that people think he's stuck up about getting into Berkeley. Bryan's a good friend. He wants to help.

"Thanks, man," Jared adds, feeling a surge of gratitude. "I'll be there." But Bryan's already hung up.

I am half an hour old, working my way through the boxes of old EPs, Halloween costumes, baby clothes. The life-size paper-maché sculpture Jared made of Abraham Lincoln in sixth grade. The chest of wool sweaters no one has worn since the Reagan years, mothballed and delicious.

Before, when Marie heard the word "breakdown," she associated it with a sudden shift – something triggered. Like a twig stepped on by a heavy boot, snapped cleanly in two. Before: whole. After: broken. But Marie's breakdown was not like that. For her, the breakdown was something that built over a matter of days and weeks and months, a gradually increasing sense of claustrophobia – compounded by guilt that she was feeling anything but gratitude for her life. Because, Marie knew, she had much to be grateful for: a loving husband, a good son, a beautiful home in a safe neighborhood. Lunches with friends at the Country Club and volunteer work at the library. She never worried about money. She and George rarely argued. She had a life people yearned for and envied. An easy life.

Maybe, she thought at first, her anxiety stemmed from Jared – the knowledge that he would be leaving them soon; moving out of the house and off to college, away to the next stage of his life, independent from them. He would not need her any longer. She felt purposeless, restless. And part of it was related to Jared, yes – but, if she was honest with herself, it had been a while since he had needed her, *really* needed her. Moving out was the final step of a process long begun.

As the weeks dragged on, the feeling within her expanded, and it was bigger than Jared, bigger than George, bigger than menopause or the onset of winter, the blossomless jacaranda trees like ghosts in the yard. She went for long walks through the neighborhood, wanting to just keep walking, away, away, away from it all. Wanting to burn everything down and start again. Renewal in having nothing. Freedom in the ashes of what used to be.

Marie heard once that if you put a frog in a pot of water that is ever-so-slowly brought to a boil, the frog will not notice the increase in temperature, and will be boiled alive without even trying to leap from the pot. Her breakdown happened when she noticed. Her breakdown was an attempt at a leap.

I bide my time, keeping quiet, gaining ground without much notice.

It is 9:32pm.

Marie lifts her knuckle to Jared's bedroom door and tentatively knocks.

"Come in."

The door whines as she opens it. Jared is flopped back on his bed, spiral notebook on his bent knees, the bedside lamp blazing a halo of light on his face.

"What are you working on?" she asks from the doorway.

"Homework. Thought I'd get something done since I'm not going anywhere."

Sometimes, when she looks at her son, Marie is amazed by how strange he seems to her. How unknowable. For nine long months, he grew inside her – she was his everything – and now. Now he humors her? Resents her? Now they are strangers who just happen to live under the same roof.

"Thank you for staying in tonight," she says.

"It's no big deal."

"I just have a bad feeling. A mother's intuition. I know you think I'm crazy…"

Marie trails off, but Jared doesn't respond. She waits a moment more, then says, "I'm going to the store to get groceries for the week."

"You're going *now*?" Jared sits up. "Is the store even open this late?"

"Till eleven. I hate to deal with the crowds."

"How long will you be gone?"

"Not long. Anything you want me to get for you?"

Jared leans back against his pillow. "Mountain Dew."

"Okay," Marie says, not even putting up a fight about the amount of sugar or chemicals in that drink, his favorite since he was a boy. She understands that Jared is bargaining with her. He is staying home tonight, and she is buying him Mountain Dew. She can do that.

"I love you," she says, and shuts the door before he can decline to say it back.

I am spurred onward by desire, not love. Need, not want. There is a difference. I do not love anything. I do not know what it means to be selfless. Yet there is honor in my pursuit: I am exactly where I am supposed to be, doing exactly what I am supposed to do. Consumption is my life's purpose. It must be. If not, why would it be such an irrepressible urge within me?

George is down the hall in his study, doing online Sudoko. Marie comes in without knocking.

"I'm going to the store," she says.

Ever since her last breakdown, she's been going to the store late at night, when no one else is there. George thought it would be good for them to shop together, or for her to go during the day or evening like everyone else, when she would have a chance to run into friends. He hates to see her withdrawing from the world like this – so scared, so on edge. But her doctor, a thick-haired pompous wearer of sweater-vests who George does not trust, sided with Marie, saying it would be best for her to avoid crowds and "anxiety-inducing situations."

"Okay," George says now, not looking up from his computer screen. "Drive safe."

"I will. See you in a little while."

"I'll probably be asleep when you get back. I'm thinking of hitting the sack soon."

"Oh. Okay, then." The hurt on her face is what George wanted, yet it brings him no satisfaction. Is this what they've come to – round after round of bruised feelings and subtle barbs?

"It's been a long week," he adds.

59

Marie nods, then leaves, shutting the door behind her. George closes Sudoko and opens his favorite porn site.

It is 9:43 p.m.

I can detect life in the layers of house below me, creaking the floorboards, rattling the pipes. But they do not frighten me. They have no idea I am here. No idea how strong I am becoming with every passing second.

Somewhere in this attic is a box that has not been opened in twenty-six years. Inside rests a wedding dress, carefully folded and wrapped in tissue paper. It is the last thing I find before everything comes crashing down.

Jared stares at his bedroom ceiling, wondering what he'll tell his parents if he gets caught tonight.

George watches the pixilated gyrating blondes, trying to fight away the image of his wife's timid, broken eyes.

Marie climbs into her Lexus with her reusable grocery bags and backs down the driveway, thinking how monstrous the house looks at night, like a dark palace against the blue-black sky. Like something out of a grim fairy tale.

It is 9:53 p.m.

In the ensuing weeks, after George and Jared's funerals, people will try to console Marie with words, facts, scientific terms. It was an electrical fire. It started in the attic. There is no way anyone could have known. It was a slow-burning, smoldering nightmare. No warning. No smoke. The ceiling just collapsed, and by then it was too late.

Nobody's fault. Just one of those bizarre freak accidents.

But Marie does not believe in accidents. Until the day she dies (February 16, four years later, her Lexus colliding head-on into a tree) she is convinced the fire is her fault. She is the reason it came into being. She is the one who left; who abandoned it all, everything, to burn.

60

It is 10:36 p.m. on Friday night. The back seat of Marie's Lexus bulges with groceries. She first glimpses the smoke from all the way down the street. She presses her foot to the gas pedal, hurrying, hurrying, her heartbeat a blur of thumping. As if a part of her knows what she will find.

Fire trucks, an ambulance, neighbors crowding the street. The choking smell of soot and ashes.

3642 Maplewood Drive, engulfed in flames.

Our lives are short. That is the nature of any existence. I know I will die before I am ready – but, then again, won't we all?

The men lift their hoses and gun me down.

Jared Sampson's Mom

She died in a car crash yesterday. She was driving down Hawthorne, past the strip mall with the Benihana's, when her Lexus unaccountably careened over the center meridian and smashed head-on into a tree.

"I just thought you should know," my mother says. My cell phone feels hot against my ear. "That poor family. It's like they were cursed. And Marie was such a nice woman." My mother sighs loudly into the phone. "I just can't believe it."

"Me neither."

"Part of me thought I shouldn't tell you. I didn't want to upset you with such horrible news. But then I realized you'd hear about it anyway on that bookface thing, and I thought the news would be better coming from me."

I'm not Facebook friends with many people from high school. If Jared were still alive I might be Facebook friends with him, but only because we were both friends with Bryan. Before the house fire, I hadn't really spoken to Jared since eighth grade, when I asked him to dance at the semi-formal and he said, "Um – no thanks, I'm okay." That was the first time I wore mascara, and Jared was the first boy I cried over in a musty, cramped bathroom stall, and I unknowingly wiped mascara-tears all over the front of my new white dress.

"It's okay, Mom," I say now. "I'm glad you told me."

"If I wear this bra, do I have to wear the matching panties?" Minnie stomps into the living room and faces us, hands on hips, posing. She is always posing. Her dark red hair hangs in loose wet ropes down her shower-damp back and shoulders. She is wearing a black bra and black panties, both edged in red lace.

Sasha and I blink at her from the couch. "I like the matching," Sasha says. "But I wouldn't feel constrained. It's not like Zack's gonna notice, he'll be so busy tearing them off

62

you."

I cross my legs and pull my phone from the front pocket of my jeans. 6:37. Zero missed calls. I haven't heard from Ben all day.

"If you want to wear the bra," Sasha continues, "it doesn't mean you *have* to wear the matching panties."

"What do you think, Di?" Minnie asks.

"What?" They're both looking at me. "Oh," I say, "I've never owned matching underwear." It's true. I get my bras on discount from Macy's and my underwear at the Jockey outlet store.

"This is my only matching set," Minnie says. "Oh, and the pink ones. But I never wear them." She stretches her arms above her head and looks down at her chest. "I like this bra, but I want to wear my zebra panties."

"Oooh, yes, do it," Sasha says, already turning back to the fabric in her lap. She is sewing red sequins one-by-one onto a white T-shirt. Watching her jab the needle through the heart of a sequin and pull the thread taut, I think of Jared Sampson's mom and the way her heart must have constricted when she drove up to her house and saw it in flames. The sort of thing you never stop seeing, even when you close your eyes, even years later.

"You know," I say, pushing myself up off the worn couch cushion. "I'm sure you can buy a shirt like that online. You don't have to go through so much trouble."

"It wouldn't be the same," she says without looking up.

Sequins spill across the cushion beside her. So many pieces. So much red. Sasha is sewing the sequins in a spiral unwinding outward from the center. She will keep sewing until the entire shirt is covered. The red catches the light and holds it close.

Jared Sampson's mom was driving home from picking up nasal decongestant at the drugstore. She had a cold; she was feeling drowsy. She closed her eyes for only a moment and then –

Jared Sampson's mom was driving home from visiting Jared's grandmother at the nursing home. She was heading down Hawthorne, past the strip mall with the Benihana's, when her cell phone rang. She reached down and fumbled through her purse, taking her eyes off the road for only a moment, and then –

Jared Sampson's mom was driving home from work, where she'd been chewed out by her boss for being late with the expense reports. She was lonely and tired and felt the beginnings of a migraine slowly building behind her eyes. If she turned the wheel a little to the right, she thought, then a hard sudden jerk to the left, and then –

The semi-formal was held the last Wednesday of the school year. There was a stalemate on the social committee between the themes "Loveboat" and "Tarzan," so the gym was decorated with pink and red hearts and green streamers. Cut-out fish swam across the walls alongside butcher-paper tigers and gorillas. I wore my new white dress with the pearl buttons down the front and my hair pinned back in a white satin barrette. Emily had pilfered mascara from her mother's makeup bag and we brushed it on our lashes in the bathroom before the dance. I had never felt so grown-up.

Emily and I danced the Macarena and the Electric Slide towards the front entrance to the gym; Jared and his friends stood at the back by the basketball hoop, talking instead of dancing. Time whirled past. Then the opening notes of an N'Sync love ballad floated from the speakers. Within moments, couples around us were pairing off, hesitantly touching each other from an arm's length away, feet shuffling in a tight circle.

"Diana," Emily nudged me. "You should ask Jared to dance."

"Oh," I said. "I don't know…"

"It's the last dance of the year. What do you have to lose?"

"I can't. I'm too nervous."

"Just do it, Di."

The chorus swelled as I began walking in Jared's direction, telling myself I could always change my mind and turn back. But I didn't. I wiped my sweaty palms on my dress and gently touched Jared's arm. He turned.

"Hi," I said.

"Hey."

"Do you, um, wanna dance?" The question hovered in the air between us. Jared glanced at his friends, then back at me.

"Um – no thanks, I'm okay," Jared said, running a hand through his brown hair. I felt like an egg yolk slipping out of its cracked shell. I slinked through the crowd of dancing bodies and hurled myself into the girls bathroom, where I plopped down on a toilet seat and sobbed. Minutes passed, I'm not sure how many, when the bathroom door opened and footsteps came in. I pulled my knees up onto the toilet and tried to quiet my sniffles, but there was a knock on my stall door.

"Are you okay in there?" a woman's voice said.

"I'm fine," I choked out.

"You don't sound fine."

"It's not a big deal."

"Here. At least let me give you a tissue."

I waited in silence, hoping she would leave, but she knocked again. "Please, honey, open up." I wiped my eyes and undid the lock.

In front of me stood Jared Sampson's mom, with her red lipstick, short blonde perm and flower-patterned capri pants. She wore a "Parent Chaperone" sticker with her name written out in green marker. Seeing her, I crumpled anew into fresh tears. "Honey, it's okay," Mrs. Sampson said. "What's wrong? What happened?"

"I asked a boy to dance," I sniffled, wiping my nose with the back of my hand. "And he said, 'No thanks.'"

"Oh, sweetheart." She handed me a tissue from her

purse. "I can't tell you how many times I heard 'No thanks' growing up."

"You did?"

"Of course! Boys can be stupid at your age. All they care about is looking cool – and dancing isn't cool to them"

"I wish I hadn't asked him."

"Don't say that – you should be proud of yourself." Jared Sampson's mom squeezed my hand. "You were brave, and this boy was silly. His loss. So move on. You don't ever have to talk to him again."

I have a toothache and my ear is itching, one of those deep inner-ear itches that you try to gouge out with a Q-tip but even that doesn't help. My bedroom window is open. The sounds outside, everyday neighborhood sounds – a burst of rap music, a car rumbling down the street, a woman pleading with her dog, "C'mon Henry, that's a good boy, you have to go potty, don't you?" – feel closer that usual. Even the wind blows more intensely, a rush of air like a sharp exhalation of breath. The room is cold. I could close the window, but then it would get stuffy.

I don't know where my roommates are. The kitchen light wavers, then blinks on. The bag of salad I bought last week is already old and mulchy, the lettuce limp, the dressing sour. I'll probably end up ordering a pizza for dinner, or maybe I'll just consume the half-empty package of Oreos lurking in the pantry. *If I eat them all now,* I think, grabbing the package off the shelf, *I won't be tempted to eat them later.*

Minnie comes home as I'm demolishing the final row. "Oooh, Oreos!" she shrieks. "Can I have one?"

I hold the tray out to her. She takes three.

"How was your date last night?" I ask.

"It was fun," she says, plopping down beside me on the couch. "We went to dinner – he paid – and then to a movie – he paid – and then he took me back to his place. He has a really nice TV in his room." Her cell phone rings, Justin Timberlake crooning a love ballad. Minnie rummages in her

66

oversized leather purse and pulls out her phone. She flips it open. "Hi babydoll! I'm so sorry I didn't call last night – I was out on a date with Zack."

She stands up and blows me a kiss before disappearing down the hall to her room. I hear her say, "It was okay, but he's not as fit as you are..." as the bedroom door clicks shut.

Minnie has been dating her "babydoll" Anthony long-distance for three years. He goes to Ohio State, where they start classes a few weeks after we do, so he always drives down to help Minnie move in and stays at our place for a week before flying out to Columbus. Usually during these visits Minnie and Anthony seem almost like one person, curled up on the couch together watching TV, holding hands to walk to the kitchen for a glass of water. But on Anthony's last visit they moved through the apartment on separate tracks. Anthony spent hours alone in Minnie's room, surfing the Internet, while Minnie grabbed coffee with friends from her yoga class. On the morning Anthony left for Ohio, they ate bowls of cereal in different rooms, and Minnie came back from the airport singing the new Fergie song instead of fighting her tears.

Still, I was surprised to log onto Facebook a week later and see Minnie listed as "Single."

"I love Anthony," she said when I asked her. "I just want to live the single life for a bit."

"So you guys broke up?"

"Well, not really. Just on Facebook. You need to be single to get dates."

"Isn't that kind of lying?"

"No. I mean, Zack knows I'm only into casual dating."

"What if he wants to get serious?"

"Then I'll end it with him. I told you, Anthony's the man I want to marry. I just want to sleep with other people in the meantime, while I'm still young."

"I can't believe Anthony's okay with this," I said.

"Why wouldn't he be? He gets to live the single life, too. We're both allowed to date three other people, and then at Winter Break we'll reassess."

I'm gonna miss you so much, Ben.

I know. But we just gotta make it to Winter Break. Then we'll have three weeks together.

Yeah.

Don't worry. We can make it work, Di. I know we can.

"Besides," Minnie continued, "there's this girl at school Anthony's really good friends with. Carissa. He talks about her all the time. I've always been suspicious there's something between them."

"Maybe they're just friends."

"Oh Diana, you're so naive sometimes."

"People can just be friends."

"Well, Anthony said he'll probably make a move on Carissa now."

"Aren't you – " I squeezed my fingers. My hands felt cold. "Isn't there a little part of you that's worried?"

Minnie tugged out her ponytail. Her hair tumbled around her shoulders like a shampoo commercial. "No," she said, smiling radiantly. "I know he loves me best."

Ben, do you love me best?

Of course I do. I love you.

But best? Do you love me best? Out of everyone?

Diana, I love you. I love you, I love you, I love you. How many times do I have to say it?

Now, I eat the final Oreo and crumple the empty wrapper in my fist. Sometimes I miss him so much it becomes a physical pressure building behind my eyes.

He answers on the second ring. "Hey babe, can I call you back? I'm at Becky's."

I can hear Becky's voice in the background, but I can't make out what she's saying.

"Sure," I say. "That's fine – okay, bye."

The driver's door crushed like a beer can. The

windshield a sickening spider web of broken glass. Blood. Her body slumped lifeless against the steering wheel.

I'm having trouble sleeping.

Ben has a paper due tomorrow. Eight pages. Twenty citations. It is 1:14 a.m.

"So what's your thesis statement?" I ask, pressing the phone against my ear, as if to press myself closer to him. "Maybe if you talk things through, it'll help clear your head."

"I don't know," he says.

"Just try. What's your thesis?"

"I mean I don't have one yet."

"You don't have a thesis?" 1:15 a.m. The paper is due in less than eight hours. Supposedly, he's been working on it all afternoon.

"I just – I'm having trouble focusing," he says. "I know what I want to say, I'm just having trouble saying it."

"You're a brilliant writer, Ben." And he is. He once wrote a short story from the perspective of the Mississippi River that had me in tears. "You're just overthinking. You're making this too big a deal."

"I know." His tone makes me think of fallen leaves mushed sadly in the gutter. "I just – every sentence I write, I see everything wrong with it. All the ways they can rip my argument apart."

"But that's how it is with writing," I say, shifting the phone to my other ear. "Every point you make can always be argued. You're gonna drive yourself crazy trying to search for some airtight argument that doesn't exist."

"You're right, you're right. I need to buckle down and *do* it." He sighs. "I'm never gonna get it done in time."

"Yes you will. You have to. You have to turn in *something*."

"You're right." He pauses. I watch the clock on the wall tick seconds away. One, two, three. "But, you know," he says, "if I don't turn it in, I'll still be okay. If I do all the other work in the class. It's not like I'm gonna flunk."

69

"Ben – "

"I'm not gonna flunk, Diana."

"Why don't you just try talking it out to me? Please. I can help."

"It's no use – it's not going anywhere. I didn't give myself enough time. And I got the book late. Remember, how the mail took forever? So I'm behind on the readings…"

Frustration burns hotly in my chest. "Maybe if you weren't hanging out with Becky all the time," I hear myself saying, "you would have it done."

His voice hardens. "What? What does Becky have to do with anything?"

"You've been spending so much time with her lately. It seems like every time I call, you're with her."

"Diana, I know you're jealous of Becky, but seriously – "

"I'm not jealous!"

" – it's kind of getting ridiculous. She's my friend, okay? You're my girlfriend. She's the one who should be jealous of you."

I know this is supposed to reassure me, but it doesn't. I pick at a scab on my arm and don't say anything.

"I mean," he continues, "it's not like you're around for me to hang out with."

"You act like that's my fault."

"It's not your fault. It's not anyone's fault. It is what it is."

Words fill my throat like grains of rice expanding in water. So many words that I can't get a single one out.

"Anyway, I'm gonna try, okay?" Ben sighs. "But I just don't think I'll finish this paper in time."

I have never felt farther from him. "Ben," I whisper. "I don't know if I can do this anymore."

"Diana?" he says after a moment. "Hello? Di? You still there?"

I met Ben at summer camp last year. We were both

counselors for the third graders, which meant we were on the same schedule for practically everything – hiking, horseback riding, swimming in the lake. Trying to keep track of sugar-crazed nine-year-olds all day made the two of us inseparable. We had secret nicknames for all our campers and swapped mealtime shifts to give each other nap breaks. I had only known him four days when he kissed me, the two of us wedged in the supply closet looking for extra Boondoggle lanyard for the campers to make key chains during arts and crafts. A week later, we were officially dating. And at the end of the summer, Ben told me he loved me.

"There's no one else I want to be with," he said as we walked hand-in-hand around the lake. All the campers had gone home; this last week was spent cleaning out the cabins and preparing the camp for its winter hibernation. "I really think we can make long-distance work."

"I do, too," I said. Looking back, I'm not sure I fully believed the words as they came from my lips, but I did love him, as wholly and deeply as you can love someone you've only known in an isolated camp-world for nine weeks. To my summer-self, armed with that steady, untested love, L.A. and Denver didn't seem far apart at all.

Then Ben went to school and met Becky in his history class. Minnie and Anthony started dating other people. Jared Sampson's mom died in a car crash. Nothing seems certain anymore.

Emily calls me. She goes by Emmi now. We were good friends all through middle school and high school, but college changes people. It changed Emily. She smokes and drinks and occasionally leaves messages on my cell phone at 4 a.m. on random weeknights. I usually can't hear much other than shouting and thumping bass music, though sometimes Emily will shout into the phone, "I loooove you, Diana! You're awesome! Don't ever change! Okay? Okay? Call me! I looooove you!"

One time I did call her, but she didn't remember

leaving the message. "I said that?" she laughed. "I was *so* wasted last night, my god."

This time she's calling because she heard about Jared Sampson's mom. "Can you believe it, Di? I can't believe it."

"Me neither."

"She was such a nice lady. Remember that time in middle school when she brought in cookies for everyone? She must have baked three-hundred snickerdoodles. It was during that week of standardized testing. She knew we all could use a cookie."

"Oh, yeah. I'd forgotten about that."

"That family was, like, cursed. Can you imagine? I can't imagine. Hey, I went home last weekend for Gunny's birthday, and guess who I ran into?"

"Ummm…"

"You'll never guess."

"Okay, who?"

"Actually, I don't even remember his name! That annoying nerdy kid – he'd play hackey-sack by himself in the corner of the caf? Eugene?"

"Erik."

"Eugene fits him better. Anyway, I saw him at the grocery store, but I just ducked my head and walked by – didn't want to get caught in some awkward conversation, you know? Ha, remember, if you went up to him he'd always try to lecture you with random facts about dolphins or some crazy shit?"

"He wasn't that bad. Didn't you kiss him at my party that one time?"

"What! No! Who told you that?"

"You did, back in high school."

"I never said that. I never would have kissed him."

"I heard he's going to Stanford now and is studying neuroscience or something crazy-smart."

The line hums quietly. "Give me a minute!" she shrieks to someone. "Hey Di," she says. "Are you going to our high school reunion?"

"What?"

"When we have our high school reunion, will you go with me?"

"Um, yeah – sure. But it's not for a while, right? I mean – "

"God, I think about myself back then and it makes me cringe. I wish I could go back to high school the way I am now. I could win Prom Queen."

"Yeah, I bet you could."

I have a four-year-old voice mail saved on my cell phone. Not anything special, really – high-school Emily calling to see how I was feeling. I was sick with the flu and missed three days of school. She went to all my classes and picked up my homework assignments and leant me season five of *Friends* on DVD. "Get well soon, Diana," high-school Emily says in the voice mail. "I missed you *sooo* much today. School totally sucks without you." When we first went away to college, I saved it on my phone so I could listen to Emily's voice in case I was ever really homesick and couldn't get a hold of her. Now, I listen to it sometimes, but only when I'm feeling particularly nostalgic. That girl on the voice mail is all I have left of my best friend.

"I talked to Emily today."

"Who's Emily?" Ben asks.

"My friend from high school. I've told you about her."

"Sorry. Her name doesn't ring a bell."

"I know I've mentioned her."

"Are we really gonna argue about this?" Ben sighs. I can hear muffled sounds in the background, but it's probably just the TV. "Okay, you told me and I forgot. My plate's been pretty full lately, you know."

My gut sinks, as it always does when his voice congeals to aloofness. "Never mind," I say.

"Babe, c'mon, don't be this way. Finish your story."

"It's not a big deal."

"Finish your story, Diana. Please."

"It's nothing – she just called because of a kid we went to school with. His mom died last week."

Something clatters in the background. "Shit," Ben says.

"Are you okay?"

"I'm fine. I dropped a glass."

"Did it break?"

"Yeah, there's glass everywhere."

"Be careful."

"Hold on a sec," he says. I count to twelve. "Sorry, I'm back. So what were you saying? Your friend's mom died?"

I wish I hadn't told him. "Not a friend, really. This boy from my hometown who I went to school with, who died right before graduation. We weren't friends or anything – "

"Wait, he died? Or his mom died?"

I can feel a headache building behind my temples. "He died back in high school. His house caught on fire, and only his mom survived. Except now she died."

"How?"

"Car crash."

"That sucks," Ben says.

"I know."

Silence. We have run out of words. I want to ask Ben if I've changed since the summer. I want to ask if he still loves me. I want to ask if he feels like something is wrong, like the world is slowly drifting apart. Inescapable currents tugging us all away from each other.

"When can I come visit?" I ask. We spent many midnight hours at summer camp, huddled on the damp ground by the mist-shrouded lake, dreaming about visiting each other at school. "You feel so far away."

"I have to check my work schedule," he says. "I'll let you know, okay?"

I dream that Jared Sampson's mom and I are at a tea party. I'm so happy to see her that I start to cry. She thinks I'm crying over something else. "Honey," she says, "it's okay. It's his loss." She pours me tea and hands me a scone. I feel better. But then I realize we're sitting in the bottom of an empty pool. The concrete walls rise up all around us. We're in the deep end. Slowly, the pool fills. Water soaks into my shoes, my socks, the cuffs of my jeans. I bite into the scone, but it's turned to plastic. The water rises past my knees, my hips. Jared Sampson's mom smiles at me, buttering a plastic muffin. "Don't worry, Diana," she says. "You don't ever have to talk to that boy again." The water is at my shoulders now. I close my eyes. It rises up past my nose, my forehead. It soaks my hair. I'm going to drown.

I wake up gasping for breath.

Moments later, Sasha prances into my room.

"You're awake!" she shrieks.

"Good morning." I rub a bit of sleep from the corner of my eye.

"How do you like it?"

"Like what?"

"My shirt! I just now finished it!" She raises her arms and turns from side to side. Her torso is a glittering sea of red.

"It's very…eye-catching," I say. In the dream, Jared Sampson's mom was wearing red lipstick. It outlined her smile like boldfaced type.

"Hey!" Minnie lounges against the doorframe. "Cute shirt, Sash. Can I borrow it for my date on Friday?"

You look good in red, Diana. You should wear it more.

I don't know, Ben. It's not really my color. Too flashy.

Red's not flashy — it's vibrant.

There's one picture of Becky on Facebook that I really hate. She's with Ben, of course. They're standing very close together. He has his arm around her, and she's wearing a red dress.

I dial Ben's number and he answers. "Listen, Ben," I say. "I don't think things are working out." He cries and begs me to stay with him, but I remain steadfast. "I know it's hard, but I really think it's for the best – "

I dial Ben's number and he answers. "Listen, Ben," I say. "This long-distance thing is just too hard." He cries and promises to try harder. He swears we can make it work. He wants me to come visit next weekend. "I don't know," I say. "I'll have to think about it – "

I dial Ben's number and he answers. "Listen, Ben," I say. "I know you're cheating on me with Becky." He cries and admits to everything. He says it was a stupid mistake. He's not seeing Becky ever again. "You, Diana," he says. "You're the one I love best – "

I dial Ben's number. He doesn't answer.

In middle school, Jared Sampson and I rode the same bus. One day in eighth grade rainclouds called a conference between fifth and sixth period, and by the end of the day the gutters were rivers. My hair was drenched walking from my locker to the bus. At my stop I climbed down the steep bus steps, gripping the railing so I wouldn't slip. Jared Sampson clambered down right behind me.

I turned and waved. "Bye, Jared!" I said, heart pounding. Before he could respond (or not respond) I ducked my head into the rain and resigned myself for a cold, wet walk up the hill to my house.

I hadn't trekked half a block when a green minivan pulled up beside me. Jared Sampson's mom rolled down the window.

"Diana, honey," she said. "Isn't your mom or dad picking you up?"

"They're at work," I said.

"Oh, sweetheart. Get in. We'll drive you home. Jared, open the door for her."

Eighth-grade Jared wore cargo shorts with lots of pockets. I thought the way his hair curled over the back collar of his shirt was cute. He had a quiet way about him. When he smiled at me, I felt a personal sense of accomplishment.

Jared heaved open the minivan door. I climbed in and slammed it shut. The radio was tuned to a classical station. Jared slouched in the middle row: a bench seat, with only room for two.

"You're half-soaked already," Mrs. Sampson said. "I've got the heater on high. Jared, make room for Diana." He drew his knees together. I plopped down beside him, slinging my bulging backpack on the floor next to my feet.

"Now Diana, remind me what street you live on?"

"Hayward. Keep going up this street and take the fourth left."

The minivan lurched forward. "Buckle up, kids!"

Jared moved his arm out of the way so I could snap in my buckle. We were sitting very close. I was acutely aware of Jared's breathing, his boy smell, his right knee inches from my left. In that moment, life was limitless. I wished I could stay in that minivan forever, warm and out of the rain, sitting beside Jared Sampson on that narrow bench seat. At one point, as we turned a corner, his body leaned my way and our knees and shoulders touched. I wanted us to just keep driving – past my house, past my street, past my neighborhood, going around lots of turns. I didn't know where we'd end up. But Jared Sampson's mom was driving, so I felt safe.

Three Sundays at The Grove

When Deepti was born in San Francisco in the summertime, her parents were living in a tiny apartment above an Indian restaurant called The Golden Sari and they were in their Hindi phase. Deepti often wondered whether the Indian restaurant and the samosas her mother craved during pregnancy influenced their sudden conversion to Hinduism. It would make sense, knowing her mother. She judged a culture based on one thing: its food. Once she found a type of cuisine she liked, she immediately embraced all aspects of that culture. Over the years she had acquired a wide mishmash of cultural affectations to match her ever-growing palate, trying on religions and customs, discarding some aspects while keeping others, as if the world were an immense shopping mall waiting to expand her cultural wardrobe. Deepti wondered, if her parents had lived above an Italian restaurant instead of "The Golden Sari," would they have had a Catholic phase? Would Deepti instead be named Mary or Teresa or Anne?

Regardless, that was twenty-one years ago and the Hindi phase was long gone – as was her father. Still, Deepti was left with two ever-constant reminders: her vegetarianism and her name, Charusheela Deepti, which roughly translates to "beautiful jewel full of light." These two things, combined with her honey-freckled skin, almond eyes, and unruly wiry curls, made her into what a classmate in high school once called a "character." It was meant as a compliment, Deepti thought; this was America, after all, where individuality is praised and prized. Still, Deepti often felt she was a part of many groups – part Asian, part black, part Hindi – and yet not *really* a part of any group. She was a one-woman species, unclassifiable.

"So what is it that makes someone an American?" the T.A. said. She stood close to the whiteboard, marker in hand, ready to write down whatever morsels of insight her students offered. No hands raised.

Deepti slouched in her chair, pulling down the hood of her sweatshirt.

"I don't think there are specific traits that make someone an American," said a boy in the front row. "I mean, we don't even all speak the same language anymore. Did you know the government is printing ballots in Spanish now?"

"Why's that a bad thing?" another boy put in. Deepti lifted her head at the passion in his tone. "That's what makes America great – there are so many different cultures living side-by-side in the same country. People still remember where they came from. They keep alive the traditions and languages of their homelands, but they also forge a new life in America. It's like when you move away from home – you don't need Mom and Dad anymore, but that doesn't mean you forget about their existence, does it?"

The room was silent save for the rapid squeaking of the T.A.'s marker on the whiteboard. After a moment she turned around, straightening her glasses. "Thank you for that, Philip," she said, addressing the second boy, who was now doodling on the cover of his notebook. Phil – that was his name, Deepti remembered now, he had sat next to her the first day of class and had leant her a pen. "So, Philip," the T.A. continued, "If I may ask, where is your family from?"

Phil hesitated, his cheeks slightly flushed. He had short-cropped blonde hair and sunglasses perched atop his head. He took them off, then slid them back on again. "Actually, I'm not exactly sure," he said. "My ancestors came here before the Revolutionary War. We don't know where they lived before then. Maybe England, Scotland – someplace like that."

It took Deepti a moment to digest his words. Since *before the Revolutionary War?* Imagine possessing such a sure foothold on American identity, having a sense of belonging so strong nobody could take it away. Not pieces of different cultures, shadows of ancestors brought to light in your name, your complexion, the shape of your eyes. Rather, wholeness.

79

"Does that mean you're not American, then?" a corn-rowed guy put in. "You just said that being American is having a sense of where you came from."

"Yeah," Deepti said. "He's American." It wasn't until twenty-six pairs of eyes turned to look at her that she realized she had spoken it out loud. Very loudly.

She cleared her throat. "Of course he's American. Just because you can't pinpoint your past doesn't mean it doesn't exist."

Phil smiled at her, and there was a warmth in his eyes that caught Deepti off guard – as if when he looked at her he didn't just see her honey-freckled skin, or kinky hair, or dark almond eyes, but rather all of her, together. A person. Whole.

For their first date, they went to The Grove, an outdoor shopping mall in West Hollywood rich with fountains, palm trees, and towering storefronts strung with white lights like gigantic gleaming pearl necklaces. There was even a trolley cavorting back and forth down the middle of the street. Deepti's ex-boyfriend, Thun, the son of a wealthy Vietnamese rice merchant, used to take her here after they had an argument. He would ask her to try on clothes and, as an apology, would go back later and buy them for her. At first it made Deepti feel cared for, but gradually the shopping excursions became more frequent, and before long wearing the clothes Thun bought made Deepti feel sick inside. That was seven months ago. Now, Thun was likely buying clothes for some other girl. Probably an Asian girl. He'd told Deepti once, "You're the only non-Asian girl I've ever dated."

"But I *am* Asian," she'd said. "You met my grandparents, Thun. I'm half-Chinese."

"Well, sure, you're *technically* Asian." He'd actually rolled his eyes. "But look at you. You're not *really* Asian. Not Asian-Asian. You know what I mean."

Deepti said no, she didn't know what he meant, and Thun said never mind, and she said what exactly were you implying, and he said just let it go damn it, and she said don't

80

yell at me, you don't have to yell, and he'd shown up at her apartment the next day with bulging shopping bags. But his comment stuck with her, buzzing at the collar of her shirt. Stinging her.

The more she thought about it, the more Deepti hated The Grove. But Phil had suggested it. "They have a great farmer's market here," he said.

"Let's go," Deepti said. Phil took her hand and led the way, only a half-beat away from skipping. He was like a child – excited about the smallest, most everyday things. They wove their way through the tented stalls, zig-zagged past the booths of bulging pumpkins and squashes, sizzling meat with peppers and onions, tubs of live lobsters, cloves of garlic hanging from the rafters alongside ribbon-tied bunches of dried flowers. People pushed children in strollers, their shopping bags swaying, jostling against each other in a pleasant Sunday-afternoon way. Phil bought Bing cherries, a loaf of cinnamon-cranberry bread, and two thick bars of dark chocolate. Then, "I'm starving!" he declared.

They found a stall selling cheap Chinese food – the Americanized version, with greasy noodles and deep-fried orange chicken that Deepti could not eat. She ordered the mixed vegetables instead, which were mundanely delicious. Deepti only ate "authentic" Chinese food when she visited her maternal grandparents in Oregon, so this was the type of Chinese food she was used to, the watered-down Americanized version she simultaneously recognized for its illegitimacy and loved for the same reason. And, while her own mother had preferred ordering from Panda Express to cooking recipes passed down through the family for generations, at least she had taught Deepti the correct way to use chopsticks. Phil was impressed.

"I'm terrible at using those," he said, gesturing with his plastic fork at the chow mein dangling off Deepti's chopsticks.

"It's not that hard," Deepti said. "Plus, I've been using them all my life. My mom's Chinese. Her parents came to America when she was just a baby."

"Really? That's cool."

Phil didn't ask for further details about her ancestry, but she told him anyway: "Yeah, and my dad's black. They met at Berkeley, in the '60s. You know – civil rights, free love and all that."

"Wow." Phil nodded, his eyebrows slightly furrowed as if he wasn't sure what to say. And what should he say? What did Deepti expect him, expect anyone, to say? The silence stretched, unbearable. Deepti felt a pit open up in her stomach, the greasy noodles sliding down her throat to gnawing emptiness.

"So you, do you speak any Chinese?" Phil asked.

"No, not really. Just little bits and phrases."

"That's still cool. Say something for me."

"Umm…let me think." In truth, Deepti could not remember a single phrase she had learned eight summers ago, when her mom went back to Berkeley in search of her "roots," or maybe Deepti's father, and Deepti spent a month living with her grandparents in New Jersey. Either way, Deepti was looking out their living room window for flashes of lightning when her mom's beat-up hatchback pulled into the driveway on a rainy Tuesday afternoon. She could tell from the way her mother heaved herself out of the driver's seat and shut the car door with the full weight of her body, as if crouching between its hinges were cockroaches that needed crushing, that nothing – and yet everything – had changed.

To Deepti, that summer was a fierce line drawn in the gravelly sand of her life, separating the way things were from the way things used to be. Her mother left as a loud voice and a flapping coat, jangling bracelets and jasmine incense – a hippie woman-child who gazed skyward with hopeful eyes, clutching a well-worn copy of *The Woman Warrior* to her breast and giving crinkled dollar bills to every homeless person she passed on the street. When she returned, she seemed audibly softer, smaller – a question mark slouched inside herself. Whatever she had gone to Berkeley looking for, she had not found it. When she came back, she stopped looking altogether.

Two months later, she began showing. Deepti's brother, Alson Jones, Jr., was born during the first whispered notes of spring. He was dark, too – darker than Deepti. Their mother said they had the same father, though she was no magician and another child didn't make Alson Jones, Sr. reappear.

Now, gazing into Phil's expectant eyes, the only Chinese word Deepti could summon was *kuei*. Ghost. Before that summer, her mother flipped through the pages of Maxine Hong Kingston's memoir every day, as if she could glean magic from the touch of her fingertips to the dusty ink on its pages. She memorized passages, quoted them aloud while they were eating breakfast or driving to school or shuffling through the aisles in the grocery store, their basket filled with hard green apples and skim milk: "'The difference between mad people and sane people is that sane people have variety when they talk-story. Mad people have only one story that they talk over and over.' That's what Brave Orchid says. She was Maxine's mother."

Deepti's mother referred to Maxine Hong Kingston by her first name, as if they were dear friends. Maxine, the writer of her mother's Bible, eventually became her invisible friend as well. The year before, when Deepti went home for Christmas break, she sometimes caught her mother muttering to an imaginary Maxine. Sensing Deepti there, her mother would abruptly turn around and smile, and pretend she was singing to herself.

"*Kuei*," Deepti told Phil now.

"*Kuei*. What does it mean?" he asked.

"Ghost," Deepti said. It was also the word they used for white people, but she did not tell him that part.

Deepti only had a handful of memories of her father. Being carried piggyback along a crowded city street, lulled by the sway of her father's gait and the strength of his sinewed

83

shoulders. The teddy bear her father won at some amusement park and gave to her, though Deepti wasn't sure she actually remembered the broad smile on her father's face as he presented the bear from behind his back. It was possible she was just imagining the memory.

Most of all, Deepti remembered lying in her bed at night, plugging her ears with her index fingers and screwing her eyes shut as her parents' arguments resounded through their tiny apartment above The Golden Sari.

"Who is she?" her mother would scream.

"Who is *who*?" her father would shout. "There's nobody else! You're crazy, Min!"

"Then explain where you disappear to all night. Huh? Huh? Tell me, Alson!"

"Maybe I *should* go find someone else – my own wife don't even trust me!"

"Just tell me where you were, or leave!"

"Fine, fine – I was at Bernie's. Okay?"

"What were you doing at Bernie's? Liar! You were not at Bernie's, don't even expect me to swallow that load of shit– "

"You know what? I really don't have to take this."

"Fine!" her mother screamed, the last time. "Then go! Just go, Alson! Go!"

"Okay. I'll go!"

"GO!"

"I'm going!" her father shouted, the last time. "Don't worry, Minjun – I'm gone!"

Deepti heard every word, despite her fingers plugging up her ears. That was the last time she heard her father's voice. To Deepti, the sharp slam of the front door was the world shattering.

"My parents are coming to visit this weekend," Phil said.

"Yeah?"

"They want to meet you."

"Really?"

"Of course! You're my girlfriend."

"I know," Deepti said. "But, I mean, it hasn't been that long."

"It's been four months."

Deepti swallowed. "It's just – that's kind of a serious step, isn't it? Meeting the parents?"

Phil smoothed his palms over his blue-jeaned thighs. "I didn't realize our relationship was such a casual thing to you."

"It's not – Phil, listen – "

"Deep, you're an important part of my life and my parents want to meet you. I don't get what's so weird about that."

"It's just…" Deepti sighed, fiddling with the zipper on her hooded sweatshirt. "Are you sure they want to meet *me*? I mean, look at me, Phil. Do they know I'm not some – some rich white sorority girl?"

"Is that how you think of me?" Phil asked quietly. Deepti could hear the hurt in his voice. "Nothing but a rich white frat boy?"

Deepti fumbled for words. "No, Phil – I'm sorry. I didn't mean that." She reached for his hand. "I would be honored to meet your parents. Really."

"You don't have to."

"I want to."

"I was thinking," Phil said, "maybe we could take them to The Grove?"

This time they did not eat at a stall at the farmer's market, but instead at a restaurant with tablecloths and linen napkins and menus written in French. *La Tomate Brulante.* They sat at a table on the patio. The sun shone brightly in Deepti's eyes, making her squint, but she thought it would be rude to put on her sunglasses. Beads of sweat coalesced on the back of her neck.

"So, Deepti, what is your major?" Phil's mother

asked. She wore her hair in a loosely coiled knot at the nape of her neck, with sideswept bangs that accentuated her high forehead. Her eyes were blue and heavily mascaraed. Only twice could Deepti remember seeing her own mother wearing make-up: when she left that summer day for Berkeley, and in the wedding photo that Deepti had uncovered, framed and dusty, in a box in her grandparents' garage.

"I'm studying philosophy," she said.

"Philosophy, eh?" said Phil's father, his tone like an elbow in the ribs. "What do you plan to do with that?"

"Well, you actually have a lot of options with a philosophy degree. Students become doctors, lawyers – "

"Law, huh?" Phil's father was a tall man, even when seated, with broad shoulders and impeccable posture and a closely cropped salt-and-pepper beard. *Is he a lawyer?* Deepti tried to remember if Phil had mentioned his father's profession. She didn't think so. They didn't talk much about their families.

"Yes, but I don't know if I want to go into law," Deepti said. "I'm thinking of applying for the Peace Corps."

"Really?" Phil's father raised his eyebrows. "I didn't know kids still did that."

"It's a very competitive program, Pop," Phil said, his hand finding Deepti's beneath the table.

Later, after a round of appetizers, salad and soup, rack of lamb marinated in lemon and garlic that Deepti had to politely refuse, and after the coffee cups and sugar spoons had been cleared away, and after Phil's father made a big show of calculating the tip for the waitress, and Deepti said, "Thank you for lunch," feeling strangely unsettled at the whole ordeal of it – later, after the meal was done, they left *La Tomate Brulante* and strolled along the fake cobblestone streets, past the stores with the big windows and the strings of pearl-lights gleaming nearly translucent in the bright sunshine. There was a bridge over a man-made pond, a gaudy fountain, a grassy park swathed with trees and a small stage set up with a band playing live music. Keyboard, drums, bass, guitar.

"Oh, I love this song!" Phil's mother said. "Remember, Jack?" She smiled at Phil's father. The four of them settled down amongst the cluster of families on the grass as the notes swelled and the pianist sang, "Hey Jude."

Deepti closed her eyes, letting the music seep into her chest, golden and warm. Phil sat beside her, his hand on her knee, singing along. Maybe she worried too much. Maybe it would all be okay.

"Hey Pop, everything okay?" Phil said into his cell phone. Deepti paused the DVD they'd rented. Phil shrugged apologetically and mouthed to her, "Sorry." Into the phone he said, "I'm glad you and Mom made it back safe."

Deepti got up to refill their glasses of water. When she returned, Phil's brow was furrowed and his voice was taut. "Pop, you're out of line – "

Deepti sat down beside him, but Phil slid his arm out from behind her and stood up. "I don't understand – " he said into the phone, slipping into his bedroom. He closed the door, but the walls were thin and Deepti could still hear his end of the conversation.

"That's ridiculous – of course she has a future. What do you mean, what is her family background? What does that have to do with anything? Her mom's Chinese and her dad's black. No, Pop, I'm not – you sound crazy, do you even hear yourself? She's not pregnant – "

Deepti stared at the frozen image on the television screen, of Angelina Jolie crouched with her back to the wall, gun poised and ready to shoot. She wanted to plug her ears with her fingers, but she had learned long ago that the words you least wanted to hear were often the most impossible to keep from hearing.

"They found her," Alson said. His voice was too calm to belong to a fifth-grader.

"Hey, bud, it's two in the morning." Deepti was still

half-asleep. "Why are you up? What's going on?"

"It's Mom. They found her."

"What?" Deepti sat up. She could feel the blood rush to her temples.

"A policeman came to our house and Grandma was crying and I heard them talking about it. I don't think I'm supposed to know."

"I'm glad you called me. It's good you called."

"She's never coming back, is she?"

"I don't think so, Al. No."

"Deepti? When are you coming home?"

Deepti stuffed a couple T-shirts into a duffel bag. Bras, panties, jeans, deodorant. Phil came up and wrapped his hands around her waist. "I'm gonna miss you," he said.

"It's only three days."

"You're sure you don't want me to come with?"

"Midterms are almost here. I don't want to burden you with this."

"I've told you, it's not a burden."

"I know, but really, Phil. This is something I need to do myself." As the words left her mouth, Deepti felt a surge of guilt – Phil was trying, wasn't he? – but he just didn't understand. He had the perfect All-American family. His mother Margaret with her blush and pearls, his father Jack with his beard and law firm. Their pre-Revolutionary-War lineage. Phil wouldn't understand a mother who one day didn't pick up Alson from school, who wasn't there when he got home, who, they later found out, didn't go into work that day, either. She just disappeared. No note, no goodbye – nothing. On the kitchen table, she left her faded, dog-eared copy of *The Woman Warrior*. That was how Deepti knew she wasn't coming back.

Deepti took *The Woman Warrior* from her bookshelf and placed it gently in her bag. "I'll see you on Sunday," she said to Phil. She kissed him, hard, closing her eyes so as not to see her mother lurking in the corner of the room, gazing at her with a ghostly vacant stare.

When Deepti left her apartment the next morning, her *kuei* mother followed, sliding across the backseat of the taxi that took them to the airport. She followed Deepti onto the plane, plopping herself down on the carpeted aisle floor beside her daughter's seat, 43C. She was oblivious to the other passengers stepping on her, grunting as they heaved bulging travel bags into the overhead compartments, and the stewardesses pushing carts right through her as she lay sprawled on her side, sleeping, her thin arms folded underneath her head. Deepti had forgotten how sharply angular her mother's elbows were, how hollow her cheekbones. Even when she was alive, she had been thin and ghostly. The last time Deepti hugged her, saying goodbye after Christmas break, she had been too scared to squeeze at all, as if the slightest pressure would cause her mother's frail bones to break.

"Miss? Chicken or pork?" The stewardess's high-heel was planted squarely through Deepti's mother's chest. She was awake now, blinking up at Deepti expectantly.

"Actually, can I have your vegetarian option?" Deepti asked. In truth, the ghostly form beside her was not new. Her mother had always been pervasively half-there. Even now, even dead, she still affected Deepti's life. Her whimsical choices, trying on religions and cultures as if she were a little girl playing dress-up, determined who she, Charusheela Deepti, was and who she would always be. Deepti shifted in her narrow seat, waiting for her mixed vegetables and rice. She would always have to ask for the vegetarian option, because of her mother.

Deepti held Alson's hand as they leaned against the boat railing, watching their mother's ashes swirl away into the dark ocean waves. Their grandparents stood a few feet away, gazing down into the water with unreadable wrinkled faces. Nobody spoke.

Deepti's ghost-mother was there, too. She had followed Deepti from the airport to her grandparents' home, standing silently in the corner as Deepti ate her grandmother's dumplings and played endless games of checkers with Alson. Her ghost-mother sat on the edge of Deepti's bed all night, and Deepti couldn't sleep. She just wanted it to be over – she wanted to say goodbye and be done with it. Now, Deepti hoped her mother's *kuei* would dive in and float away with her ashes.

She didn't. But as her ashes disappeared, ocean water seeped into her clothes and weighed down her hair, spilling out of her eyes and causing her feet to squish in her shoes as she walked. Her mother, the drowned ghost. Deepti had stuffed *The Woman Warrior* into the pocket of her coat before they left her grandparents' house, in case she needed it at the funeral. She wanted to throw it into the ocean's choppy waves. Feeling the cover's flimsiness between her fingers, she almost pulled it out. But she couldn't. She couldn't just throw it away, not like that, not with her ghostly mother standing beside her and reproaching her with vacant eyes. Eyes that knew nothing and yet also seemed to know everything – everything, at least, that mattered. Everything Deepti feared. She looked into her mother's ransacked stare and saw a future chosen and waiting for her that she never wanted to claim. Deepti did not want to be her mother's substitute. She gripped the railing tighter.

"Ow!" Alson said. "You're hurting my hand!"

"Sorry," Deepti said. They turned away from the railing as the boat headed back to shore. Deepti's other hand hung limp and empty at her side. She wished Phil were there.

On her way back to school from the airport, Deepti stopped at The Grove. It was a Sunday, and families milled about. The band was back, though the bassist was out sick, the singer informed them between songs. Deepti leaned against a tree and listened to "Piano Man" and "Your Song." She left before they played "Hey, Jude."

The trolley was parked at a stop, so Deepti got on. She let her arm dangle off the side and savored the breeze against her face. Her ghost-mother sat beside her, dripping wet, muttering to herself or maybe to Maxine. Her voice was the unintelligible whisper of dried leaves.

Deepti stayed on until the last stop, by the farmer's market. Her mother followed. Deepti strolled past rows and rows of stalls, the striped tents selling gyros and rogan josh, pot stickers and polenta. Finally, she came upon what she wanted. "Big Billy's Burgers!" a sign proclaimed, strung across the front of the stall. "America's Best!" Deepti could smell meat sizzling from the grills behind the register.

"One cheeseburger, please," she told the cashier. And, six minutes later, she had an All-American burger in her hand. Nobody stopped her. Nobody could tell she had never before done this in all her life. Deepti sat down at a grease-streaked table with hard plastic chairs. There was a sticky pool of soda left from someone's spilled drink; she wiped it up with a napkin. Her ghost-mother sat down across from her. Deepti met her mother's eyes as she brought the burger up to her lips and took a bite.

It tasted strange, a taste Deepti would associate forever afterwards with forgiveness. She took bite after bite, knowing that within an hour she would be kneeling in front of a toilet in a public bathroom stall, her body repelling this foreign substance, poison to her innocent herbivorous stomach. Yet she kept eating, not really tasting anymore, just chewing and swallowing, swallowing and chewing. Thinking. About the way her mother used to sing her to sleep when she was little, a lullaby, *Just let the west wind carry your cares away, Wei shenme? Mei guanxi.* About how her mother had been found curled up underneath the fire escape beside The Golden Sari restaurant, not breathing but with a peaceful expression on her face. Deepti chewed and swallowed, swallowed and chewed, thinking finally about Phil, his hand on her knee, the way he smiled at her and she felt her own wholeness expanding inside her ribcage like a hopeful balloon.

When she had licked every morsel of meat and fat from her fingers, Deepti scrunched up the wrapper in her fist and tossed it at the nearest trashcan. She unzipped her duffel bag and took out *The Woman Warrior*. Always she was surprised at how small it was, how little it weighed. You could carry it around with you all day, in your purse, your pocket. So light a ghost could carry it. Deepti set the book carefully down on the table, smoothing the cover flat. When she got up to leave, her mother did not follow.

The Stars in Illinois

It's only early June, but the heat feels like August. Eleanor and Sasha sit on the front steps of the old Victorian-style house in downtown Los Angeles, drinking homemade margaritas and watching the daylight drain away to dusk. Sasha slaps a mosquito away from her sweat-sticky thigh. She has long thin arms and skinny ankles and wire-straight hair that sometimes looks brown and sometimes looks auburn, depending on the light.

"Damn it," she says.

"What?" Eleanor has full eyebrows and a tiny diamond stud in her left nostril. She favors sundresses and wears her hair pinned up with silver barrettes. In high school a boy told her that she had "perfect breasts" because they fit perfectly in his hands like two firm oranges. Now she thinks of him every time she eats an orange.

"I meant to stop at the 7-Eleven," Sasha says. "I wanted to buy a lotto ticket."

Eleanor checks her watch. "You'd better hurry, if you want to get it before the drawing. It's almost six now."

Sasha swats at the air. "Naw, it's okay. I don't feel like walking."

"I can drive you," Eleanor says.

"You can't drive."

"I can drive." She holds up her margarita cup. "This is only my second."

"It's fine. There's always next week," Sasha says, working her fingers through her hair to massage her scalp, searching for lumps. She is terrified of dying. So terrified that she sometimes thinks she might as well kill herself and get it over with.

Eleanor gazes out at the pink smear of sunset caught between buildings. "There aren't really sunsets in L.A.," she says. "Daylight just...slips away." She is thinking of Illinois. As a child she would sometimes grow anxious, gazing up at the full expanse of sky, trying to grasp where it ended. Illinois

93

sky isn't like L.A. sky. Illinois sky doesn't end. It stretches at the horizons to a blurred uncertain line. So much sky. Two years ago, when she first moved to L.A., Eleanor would sometimes spend hours online, clicking through photographs of cornfields and rivers. But you can't capture the sky in a photograph, not truly. The sky is what she misses most.

"If I won the lottery," Sasha says, "I would buy this house so we didn't have to pay rent all the time. Paying rent sucks."

"You'd buy this house?" Eleanor asks. "This house of all houses?"

Sasha half-turns to gaze at the eaves, paint peeling like a bad sunburn. "I've grown fond of it, I guess," she says. "I like this porch. And the music-note wallpaper in the hallway. And I like how the honeysuckle grows up under my window."

"My window doesn't get honeysuckle," Eleanor says.

"Plus, if I bought it, it would be mine. That would be enough to make me love it."

"Then you could live anywhere, is what you're saying. As long as you own the house you live in. You can love anywhere."

"I guess so," Sasha says. She takes a pondering sip of margarita. Inside her room, on her bedside table, rests a bottle of pills and a glass of water. "But I do really like this house."

Eleanor stretches her legs out in front of her. She hasn't shaved in a couple days and dark nubby hairs are visible on her knees and shins. The heat makes her legs itch. "If I won the lottery, I wouldn't live in L.A.," she says. "I'd buy a house somewhere far away."

"Where?"

"I don't know. A small town somewhere."

"Let me guess: Illinois?"

"I'm just saying. Someplace people actually know their neighbors. Around here, you say hi and people look at you like you're crazy."

"But is it really like that in Illinois?" Sasha asks. "Everyone's friendly? Everyone bakes casseroles and apple pies?"

"My mom makes green bean casserole."

"No pie?"

"Well, sometimes, on holidays." Eleanor leans back on her elbows. She knows Sasha is making fun of her, but she takes the bait anyway. "Pecan pie. My Aunt Susan makes the best pecan pie. She won a ribbon at the country fair."

"The country fair!"

"What's wrong with the country fair?"

"Nothing's wrong," Sasha says. "It just sounds…quaint."

"L.A. has a fair, doesn't it?"

"Not a quaint little country fair, that's for sure."

Eleanor wrenches a pack of Malboros from her jeans pocket. Sasha watches Eleanor search her other pockets for her lighter. There are so many ways to die. Lung cancer. Skin cancer. Fire. Car crash. So many uncontrollable ways. Sasha exhales a drawn-out sigh that turns into a yawn. "God," she says. "I hate paying rent. I feel like all my money goes towards rent. I mean, *all* my money."

"That's for sure." Eleanor, lighter found, tips her pack and daintily pulls out a cigarette with the tips of two fingers. "Do you mind?"

"Of course not," Sasha says. "You don't have to ask."

Eleanor smokes when she drinks and when she's stressed. This afternoon brought yet another no-call-back in a long string of call-backs she hasn't gotten. She didn't expect it to be this hard. Everyone said it would take time, and yes, she expected it to take some time – but *two years*? Two years and nothing more than a handful of student films and background bit parts and one shitty half-line ("Mmm, cinnamon") in a gum commercial? Sometimes the embarrassment felt so big it eclipsed everything else. Her identity nothing more than a tired cliché: the small-town Midwest girl who moves to L.A. to become an actress,

95

squeezing in auditions between her double-shifts as a waitress. Everyone was tired of that story. Especially Eleanor. *If I don't land something in the next three months,* she thinks now, *I'm moving back home and getting a real job.* She turns her face to blow the smoke away from Sasha. She knows cigarette smoke gives Sasha a headache, even though Sasha, a jubilant martyr, makes a point not to complain.

Sasha gulps her margarita. She shifts her body slightly away from Eleanor's but doesn't say anything, trying not to think about the secondhand smoke wafting into her lungs. She believes friends make sacrifices for each other. She believes sacrifices are what make friendships stronger. Like a bird culling thread and twigs to build a nest, but in reverse. Casting away in order to build.

Eleanor takes a drag of her cigarette, thinking of her high school friend Bella, who taught her to smoke. They haven't talked in years. Eleanor believes friendships are a matter of convenience and circumstance. Eventually, she or Sasha will move away. Drift apart. Get sick of each other. And then this, all of this – the margaritas, the lotto tickets, the lazy spirals of conversation – will end. It is inevitable. None of Eleanor's friendships have lasted as long as she had wanted them to. Eleanor is careful to turn her face away from Sasha when she exhales, so as not to speed up the decline.

"Hey Eleanor?" Sasha says suddenly. "If I buy a lotto ticket and it's a winner, I want to split some of the money with you."

"Thanks, Sash. That's sweet."

"No, seriously. Listen. If I die or something, like before I get the winnings, make sure you get some, okay? Don't let my parents take all the money."

Eleanor leans back on her elbows. The clouds, limned with purple, look bruised. All the ice in her margarita has melted. "Okay, Sash," she says. "What's wrong?"

"Nothing." Last week, Sasha took the bottle of painkillers from her medicine cabinet and placed them on her bedside table. Every morning when she wakes up, the pills are the first thing she sees. When she drives home from work in the evening, she considers how easy it would be to turn the wheel ever so slightly, to lean into oncoming traffic like lovers lean towards each other at a cocktail party.

"Come on," Eleanor says.

Sasha sighs. Her fingers thread through her hair and massage her scalp. "I think," she says, "that I'm gonna die soon."

If Eleanor were not Eleanor but someone else, she might laugh uncomfortably and change the subject. Or she might think Sasha is being purposefully melodramatic and try to brush it away with facts: she is only twenty-three, she eats healthy greens, she wears her seatbelt. If Eleanor were Sasha's mother, she would jump straight to alarm and ask what's wrong, is she depressed, is she eating enough?

But Eleanor is Eleanor. She tips ash from her cigarette into the rosebushes and asks, "Why?"

Sasha stretches out her legs, almost knocking over her empty plastic cup. "I've just been thinking about it a lot lately. Death. It's always…there. At the back of my mind. It didn't used to be there. I mean, it was there sometimes, I guess, but not that often. Not always like it is now."

"What's changed?"

"I don't know," Sasha says. She didn't expect it to be like this. Everyone said she would be a good teacher. She thought she could actually make a difference, even a small difference, even to just one kid. But she is a failure. Her students all hate her. When she turns to write on the whiteboard they whisper and titter to each other, and when she poses questions for discussion they stare at her blankly. No one raises a hand. Middle school kids are supposed to like their teachers. English is supposed to be a subject the kids look forward to. There are no wrong answers in English class. If you don't have something to say you can make something up. It's not like she has been assigning much homework, either – just the typical vocabulary exercises and a book report every other month.

"Did I ever tell you about my Death Dream?" Eleanor asks.

"No," Sasha says.

"When I was in seventh grade, I had a recurring dream that I drowned. There was this pond by my house that I used to swim in a lot. I loved it there. But in my dream, this whirlpool started in the center of the pond, and no matter how hard I swam for the shore, I felt myself being pulled under the water." Eleanor remembers the fear that gripped her chest and limbs as her dream-lungs filled with water. She hadn't felt calm like everyone says you feel right before you die. She felt panicked and scared.

"I was terrified to go to sleep because I died every night in my dream," Eleanor continues. "Finally my parents took me to a shrink."

Sasha frowns. "I thought you couldn't die in a dream. I read somewhere that if you die in your dream, then you actually die for real in your sleep."

"There's no way they could know that," Eleanor says. "You can't know what someone was dreaming when they died."

"I'm just saying, I read it somewhere. In a magazine."

"Well, I died in my dream."

"So what happened?" Sasha asks. "Did you go to Heaven?"

"No, it was just dark. Dark and quiet. And then I'd wake up." Eleanor stubs out her cigarette. She drops the butt into her empty plastic cup. "Anyway, it stopped after a couple months. The shrink said it was tied to my parents' divorce."

A fly hovers around their sticky cups. Sasha swats it away. "See, that makes sense," she says. "Part of what scares me is I can't think of a trigger. There's no reason I should be obsessing about death."

Eleanor sits quietly. She is the type of person who can keep eye contact for a long time. Sasha is the type of person who gets uncomfortable and looks away.

Sasha looks away. "I figure it means I'm gonna die soon," she says. "It's a premonition."

"Maybe it's the opposite," Eleanor says. "Like how a watched pot never boils."

"Huh." With her index finger, Sasha lightly traces around the small scar on her thigh she got from climbing a chain-link fence in grade school. There were no trees, so Sasha climbed fences. "You mean, I won't die if I'm too busy thinking about dying."

"Yeah, I guess." Eleanor smiles like a lady in an old painting. Her lips aren't really smiling, but her eyes are.

"What?" Sasha says. "What are you thinking about?"

"Nothing."

"Are you laughing at me? You're laughing at me."

"No, Sash," Eleanor says. "I was just thinking of my shrink."

"Your shrink?"

"Of what my shrink would say."

"What shrink?" Sasha leans forward, elbows on knees. "You don't go to a shrink."

"My old shrink, the one my parents sent me to. Because of my Death Dream."

"Oh," Sasha says. "What would he say?" The sky is steadily losing color. Above them, the moon is an orange.

Eleanor lights another cigarette. The moon is a perfect breast. "She would say, the question becomes: if you're constantly worried about death, are you really living?"

"No." Sasha rubs her eyes. "That's the answer, right? 'No, so I should stop worrying and start living!' Right?"

"There's no answer. It's just what my shrink would say."

"Do you think she's right?" Sasha asks. "Is that the answer?"

Eleanor exhales, a perfect trail of gray smoke. She doesn't say anything.

Her recurring dream wasn't really because of her parents' divorce. Her parents had been fighting bitterly for months. The divorce wasn't much of a surprise.

Eleanor first dreamt of drowning on a Wednesday in late November. That day, her best friend Mariah Quinn inexplicably untangled herself from Eleanor and retangled herself with Veronica Cross. "Sorry, Eleanor," she said. "Bus seats only hold two." Seventh-grade Eleanor walked numbly to the back of the bus and slumped down in her seat, hiding behind her backpack, crying tears into her lunchbag. She and Mariah had been best friends since kindergarten, when they both caught the chicken pox at the same time. They sat next to each other on the bus, ate lunch together, had slumber parties on the weekends. How quickly everything could be swept away.

Eleanor leans sideways against the porch railing. Between the clamor of buildings, a few stars press through the smoggy night sky. Suddenly, she points. "Hey, Sash. Make a wish."

"I thought you only wish on shooting stars," Sasha says, thinking of Bobby Meyers, the lanky blonde boy her teenage self wished for and wished for.

"In L.A., you should wish on any star you can find," Eleanor says.

Sasha tilts her face up to the sky. In ninth grade, she wore the same blue polka-dotted headband for two months because she was wearing it when Bobby Meyers asked for her phone number, and some part of her thought he would only call if she kept wearing it. The white polka-dots gradually turned gray, and then the cloth at the ends of headband began to fray and unravel from the plastic. Sasha stopped wearing it. Bobby Meyers never called. Still, Sasha knows she will keep the bottle of pills and the glass of water on her bedside table, a comfort, a superstition, like the dream catcher hanging above Eleanor's bed across the hall.

"We do too have stars in L.A.," Sasha says, pointing. "Look! Right there."

"Those aren't real stars," Eleanor says. "Not like Illinois. You should see the stars in Illinois."

The night before she left for L.A. to become a famous actress, Eleanor slept outside in the bed of her dad's pickup truck. She found the Big Dipper and Orion's Belt and searched the sky for shooting stars. None came. Or perhaps the sky was too big, and she missed them.

Living Alone

The thing about living alone is, you've got no one to scratch your back. If it's a whisper of an itch, a fleeting thing, it can usually be taken care of by leaning casually against a doorframe and swaying back and forth. Which can actually be quite nice, scratching your back against a doorframe, especially if while you're doing it you close your eyes and pretend you're a willow tree in the wind, swaying, swaying. Of course you don't look like a willow tree in the wind. You look like an insane person. But the thing about living alone is, there is no one around to see you.

But let's say you have a more stubborn itch, like maybe you went to a party at your boss's house and it was held on a Sunday afternoon in early September, and everyone was outside in the backyard because it was such a beautiful day and only the slightest bit muggy, and maybe your mouth was tired of talking about grown-up things so you sat in the grass with the children and knotted the throats of dandelions together in long, looping chains, and maybe you were wearing a halter top or a backless sundress and you didn't even notice the bugs until you got home and felt the angry bumps all over your back, especially in the middle part of your back where your arms, even if you have abnormally long arms, can't reach.

If that happens, and you live alone, the best thing to do is to strip off all your clothes and turn the shower on lukewarm and let the water beat down upon your itchy back, and you can even close your eyes and pretend it's a person there, gently scratching your itchiness away. In fact, it's good you live alone because a person's general tolerance for back scratching wears thin after only a few minutes, but you can stand under the shower for a long time. You can stand under the shower until the water turns from lukewarm to kind of cold to so cold you can't stand it any longer. And if, when you step out of the shower, you drip a trail of water on the floor all the way from the bathroom down the hall to your

102

bedroom, you won't have to worry about anyone slipping on it, or asking you to clean it up, or doing that annoying roommate martyr routine of cleaning it up without saying anything to you but adding a little checkmark to the running tally in their head of All The Ways In Which You Are a Horrible Human Being.

I once dated a guy named Phil who was partly deaf in his right ear. At the time, I didn't have a car, and he didn't like me driving his car, so whenever we went anywhere he did all the driving. Sometimes, on the freeway, he'd roll down the windows so the air flapped around us like birds' wings. I'd be halfway through a convoluted story when he'd glance at me, a placid nonexpression on his face, and I'd realize I'd been talking and talking and talking and talking and he hadn't heard a single word.

When I moved away to college, I missed my mother a lot, but I didn't want her to know I was missing her because I felt like then she would win. I don't know what game we were playing, but it seemed important, and the rules were very clear to me. If my mother knew how much I missed her, knew about the cloying homesickness twisting my insides like the stomach flu, something between us would change. So, whenever I wanted more than anything to call her, I would eat instead. I would eat whatever I could find nearby with the lowest nutritional value. *See,* I would tell myself, *this is the best. Mom would never let you eat Skittles and Cheese-Whiz for dinner.* Eventually the homesickness would morph into normal, food-induced stomach pains, and then I would feel better.

The thing about living alone is, you can walk around naked and eat dinner naked and dust the bookshelves naked. You can stand naked in front of the mirror with your hands on your hips and your hair in a towel turban and flirt with your foggy reflection. You can sing naked karaoke. Out of all the karaoke songs in the world, you can choose "My Heart

Will Go On" by Celine Dion and since you live alone no one will be there to groan at you and roll their eyes and pretend to vomit.

"But being naked is better when you're naked with someone else," says my friend Minnie, who was named after the mouse, and who has lived with Craig for one year and five months. Before Craig she lived with Roger, and before Roger she lived with Anthony, and before Anthony she lived with two other girls in an apartment during college.

"You don't know the first thing about living alone," I say.

Minnie thinks I mean it as a compliment. "Thank you," she says, smiling at me.

Whenever Minnie smiles her eyes get squinty. I have known her for seven years and I have never seen a wide-eyed Minnie smile, not even when she is drunk or surprised or trying to look good for a photograph. In photographs, it always looks as if she is squinting directly into the sun.

I glance out my kitchen window and there she is, Michelle, walking down the sidewalk, around towards my front door.

Actually the person walking past doesn't look anything like Michelle. Her hair is short and her face is pinched.

But in my mind, she is Michelle, coming around my house to knock on my front door, wanting something from me, wanting to talk to me. I leave my oatmeal half-cooked and duck into my bedroom, and once I am in my bedroom I head straight for my closet. I slide the door shut behind me. I sit there for a while, listening to my own breathing, as I wait for the knock to come on my front door.

It never comes.

Michelle must have changed her mind and turned around. Which is a relief, really. I meant it when I said I never wanted to talk to her again.

The thing about living alone is, you can go days without talking to anyone. Like maybe when you leave work on Friday you say, "Goodbye" to the person the next cubicle over from you, but then your best friend is away for the weekend with her boyfriend at a Bed & Breakfast in Carmel, and the staff at Cypress Gardens don't like for your mom to talk to you on the phone because of what happened the last time, so maybe you spend the whole weekend watching *Saved By The Bell* reruns in your bathrobe covered with kittens, and you go into work on Monday and Emily the next cubicle over from yours asks, "How was your weekend?" and when you say, "Oh, fine," your voice is rough and croaky because it hasn't been used in a while.

It took a long time for me to break up with Phil. It took a lot of practice. We'd be driving down the freeway, the windows cracked a few inches, the breeze like the muffled applause of a crowded room, and I would say to Phil, "You know, maybe we should break up."

I'd say, "This isn't working for me anymore."

I'd say, "We're just too different."

One time, Phil glanced over and saw my lips moving. "What?" he asked.

I shook my head, retreating, not ready. "Nothing," I said. "Just talking to myself."

Phil smiled, reached over and squeezed my knee. Three months later, after our relationship imploded in an Applebee's parking lot, he said, "You know, I've seen this coming for a long time." And I thought about all our car rides and I wondered if maybe I was the one who was missing something.

When my mother began to lose her mind, I took a week off work to help her get moved into Cypress Gardens. I was anxious on the plane ride there, full of nervous energy. I kept getting up to stretch my legs, pace the aisle, use the tiny plane bathroom. But when I met my mother at her house, at the old brick house with the wide yard I'd grown up in, everything was as it always was. She seemed fine, perfectly lucid, her hair neatly parted and brushed as always, her lipstick perfectly applied. She thought Cypress Gardens was a nice hotel we were going to for a vacation. She looked around her new one-bedroom apartment, with the heavy curtains and the thick carpet, and said, "My goodness, Alina. Are you sure you can afford this?"

When I left, I hugged her fiercely and said I'd be back soon. The air was cold and burned my cheeks, and tears blurred my vision.

They found the brain tumor after my mother became convinced I am not her real daughter but rather an alien life-form impersonating myself.

"Give me back my Alina!" she screamed into the phone the last time I called.

"Mom, it's me."

"You're a liar! Don't try to trick me! Where is she? What did you do with her?" Then she was screaming my name, over and over. The nurses had to sedate her.

I was supposed to fly out three weeks ago to see her. I got all the way to the freeway exit for the Burbank airport but then I couldn't go any further. I kept driving, four exits, ten exits, thinking of the way my mother used to stir sugar packets into her iced tea, delicately, the spoon never once clinking against the glass. At the fourteenth exit, I got off, turned around, and drove back home.

The thing about living alone is, you don't have to worry about coming home to your roommate having sex on the living room couch. *You* can be the one having sex on the living room couch. Or at least making out intensely on the living room couch and then moving to your bedroom for the sex part.

I have not met my lover yet, but he is out there, somewhere, so I prepare my apartment for his arrival. I buy a brand-new couch with bright red cushions and a soft brown blanket and casually mismatched pillows that I actually spent twenty minutes deliberating about in the Home Décor aisle of Target. I frame black-and-white, slightly out of focus photographs and hang them on the walls. I buy a potted begonia for my windowsill.

The first man who witnesses my transformed living room is my neighbor, Kyle, and his cat named Oliver. Kyle seems like a nice enough person, but he laughs too loudly at his own jokes and his eyes are set very far apart, and whenever I talk he looks at the wall behind me instead of at my face, which is disconcerting and causes me to lose my train of thought.

"This is a nice couch," Kyle says, running his hand along the plush fabric.

"Thank you."

"Feels like a towel."

"Pardon?"

"It feels like a brand-new towel."

"Oh. Um, thank you," I say, trying to meet Kyle's eyes.

"Where'd you get it?" He addresses the wall behind me.

"The furniture outlet on Harrison." His gaze so intent that I turn, half-anticipating a bloom of mold or a giant, hairy-legged spider. But there is nothing. Just a wall painted white.

Meanwhile, Kyle is asking me another question. I can tell it's a question by the way his voice raises at the end, but I have not grasped a word.

Kyle stares at the spot on the wall behind me expectantly.

"What?" I say.

He leans in and kisses me hard on the mouth. I kiss him back for a few seconds, because it feels good to be kissed, but then I remember this is Kyle doing the kissing and I push him away. He fixes the wall behind me with a confused and slightly hurt expression.

"I have a boyfriend," I say, wiping my mouth with my sleeve. In the corner, Oliver is swatting my begonia with his paws. "Stop it, Oliver."

Kyle picks up Oliver like a rag doll and swings him over one shoulder. "You should have said something."

"His name is Nathaniel. We met at the library." Which is true. I went to the library during my lunch break from work and checked out a collection of short stories by Gabriel García Márquez. I intended to read one story every night before bed, and in this way I would Improve Myself.

I checked out the book seven weeks ago, but it's still lying there on my nightstand. I only finished half of one story. I keep going back to the library to renew it. You're only supposed to renew books twice, but Nathaniel lets me renew and renew. He always smiles at me as he scans the barcode, a small smile, secretive. As if we're in on something together.

His name probably isn't even Nathaniel. It's just the name I gave him. To me, he looks like a Nathaniel. He looks like someone who knows things.

My mother met my father on an airplane to Chicago. She was flying there to visit her older sister in college. My father was flying there on business. My mother said he coaxed her into conversation with a corny joke about an elephant in a fridge. "He waited to laugh until I did," she said. "I liked that. Your father had a very nice laugh."

They wrote letters, and two months later when she graduated high school, my mother moved to San Francisco, where my father lived, to go to college. She dropped out after only one semester and married him. He died when I was fourteen. She never remarried.

When Michelle told me she was moving out, her face had a blankness to it, a coldness. I felt as if she'd punched me. We'd been living together for four years, since right after college – first a dumpy, tiny flat in Venice Beach, then a bigger apartment in Brentwood. We'd bought furniture together. We'd picked out dishware. We decorated for holidays. I knew one or the other of us would move out eventually, but I didn't expect it to be like it was – Michelle's sudden, casual announcement, like she was telling me she forgot to get peanut butter at the grocery store. I'd assumed that when one of us decided to move out, there would be crying over bottles of wine, tight hugs, fierce promises to come visit, to stay in touch always, always.

It was terrifying, that something I'd felt so sure and safe about could end so abruptly. A light switch flicking off. What about all the hours we'd spent talking at the kitchen table, *our* beat-up kitchen table we'd salvaged from that yard sale in Little Tokyo? What about all those late nights we'd turned on the stereo and danced around the living room until we collapsed? What about our joined routines, our rituals, our inside jokes, our encyclopedic data bases of minute facts about each other – Michelle's fear of snails, my love of all things polka-dotted; Michelle's fifth-grade school picture with the gum in her hair, my dime-sized knee scar from a childhood skating accident. Didn't all that count for *something?* Because it should. I felt sure it should.

But, from the way Michelle was acting, it seemed I was nothing more than a roommate, flung into her life by circumstance, and just as indifferently tossed away. When I came home from work, her bedroom door was often shut; boxes began to spawn in the living room and the kitchen, slowly filling with her things. She tried to claim some of the things we'd bought together, an argument that ended with me weeping, clutching a blender to my chest, screaming that I wouldn't let her have it.

"Jesus, Alina," Michelle said, her mouth cinched tightly in disgust. "Fine, take the fucking blender."

As soon as she said that, I couldn't bear to hold it any longer. I threw the blender across the room and told Michelle I never wanted to see her again.

I began to question all my relationships. I picked fights with Minnie. I grew suspicious of Phil. Maybe he was hiding something, too. Maybe he secretly despised me. Maybe, I thought, I should break up with him before he could break me.

The thing about living alone is, there is always too much food. The people who designed food packaging did not consider those of us who live alone. You can never drink a whole carton of milk before it spoils. You can never eat a whole loaf of bread before it molds.

At the grocery store, I splurge on fancy whipped cream cheese, even though I only eat bagels occasionally. Michelle was the one who loved bagels. Bagels and lox. Sometimes on Sundays she'd come home with a paper bag from Noah's Bagels, filled to the brim. And we'd eat them. The ones we didn't eat, we'd tear up into little pieces and feed to birds at the park. Food never spoiled when I lived with Michelle.

One time, as we drove down the highway with the windows cracked and flies occasionally smattering the windshield like clouds of regret, I told Phil I loved him. He turned towards me, grinning widely. He said, "Did you see that Billboard we just passed? Someone graffitied a mustache on Sarah Palin."

After I graduated college – Art History major – I had trouble finding a steady job. I worked for a few months as an English tutor, a film gopher, a smoothie barista. My mother wanted me to move back home to Sunnyvale. She didn't think Los Angeles was a civilized place to live. "You'll never find a good husband there," she said. "Full of gangs and drug dealers."

I told her my drug dealer happened to be very nice, thank you very much. She sniffed dismissively. She was never one to laugh at my jokes out of obligation. I sent her pictures of me and Michelle – standing proudly in our newly furnished apartment, smiling in the foamy waves at the beach. Still, every time I called home, my mother's first question was if I'd met someone.

"I worry about you, Alina," she'd say. "I don't want you to end up alone."

"I won't."

"You don't understand, baby girl. It's the worst kind of emptiness, living alone."

"I won't end up alone," I'd tell her. "I promise."

When I wake up, my eyes feel scratchy and a bug bite on my elbow itches like hell. I know it is going to be a mustard yellow, sweaty armpits kind of day.

It is a Saturday and I have no one.

Nathaniel isn't at the Circulation Desk, and since it is a mustard yellow day I don't want to push things by wandering around looking for him. Instead, I head over to the children's section with the giant wooden whale you can read inside, and pick out books for my future children. Which is pretty pointless, I know, because I might very well never have children, or if I do have children by the time I have them there will be a whole slew of new books to read to them, and I immediately forget all the titles of the books I do look at because I don't write them down. I do remember one has a porcupine on the cover.

I browse through Modern Fiction and New Releases. I pick books up and put them back down. Their plastic covers are greasy under my fingers. Or maybe it's my fingers that are greasy. I wipe them on my jeans, glance over at the Circulation Desk. Still no sign of Nathaniel. An old lady with purple hair and tiny reading glasses perched delicately on her nose is helping a mother and her little girl check out a stack of picture books. I've never seen this old lady before. Anger, irrational anger, pulses through me. I picture popcorn filling up a bag in the microwave. That is what my insides feel like. I hurry to the exit, yank open the heavy oak door, and there is Nathaniel, standing right in front of me, close enough to kiss.

111

At the sight of him my insides light up. He should be able to see my body glowing through my sweater.

Sometimes, I am a fish who opens her mouth and no words come out. I open my mouth. No words. I close my mouth.

"Hi," Nathaniel says. He is already moving past me, into the warmth of the library, to his home at the Circulation Desk. I want to tell him that I am in love with the way he holds his coffee cup. With the little mole on his chin. With his unevenly cuffed shirtsleeves. Instead, I say a lit-up "Hi!" but he is already past me.

My heart is filled with seeing him.

I never want to see him again.

Outside, the air is cold and burns my cheeks, and the wind blurs the world as I make my way towards my car.

Minnie and I meet for lunch at The Urth Caffé so she can tell me about her trip to Carmel. She shows me pictures on her digital camera, the two of us leaning in close to the tiny screen. Minnie's face smells powdery in a pleasant way. I want a powdery face. My face feels greasy and porous in an unpleasant way. All the pictures of the ocean make me want to drink water, and all the water I drink makes me have to pee.

"I'll be right back," I say, scooting back my chair and standing up.

I am only gone a few minutes, but when I return, Michelle is in my seat, scooted up close to Minnie, peering down at the tiny digital camera screen. I have a strange sense of déjà vu, or maybe it's more of an out-of-body-experience – as if I have stumbled upon a different version of myself, in a different version of my life.

I step backwards, bumping into a waiter. His carefully balanced tray wobbles but he steadies it. "Sorry," I say, fleeing out the back exit. I wish I were wearing a billowy silk scarf. That I had something billowing out behind me to announce the absence of my presence.

On the day of the big move, I refused to help
Michelle carry her boxes down to her friend Steve's van. I
stayed in my room, the door locked, blasting the Ramones on
my stereo. We did not say goodbye. If she knocked on my
bedroom door, I did not hear it. When I finally emerged that
night, the apartment felt like a tomb.

I called Phil and told him how empty the apartment
was. "It's so lonely in here," I said. "It feels so big. Like I'm
living inside a whale's mouth."

I wanted Phil to ask what kind of whale, but he
didn't. He just said he'd be right over. I waited for him in the
living room, sitting on the edge of the coffee table because
Michelle had taken the couch. When he knocked on the door,
I knew it was him – but part of me still leapt inside, thinking
of Michelle, of all the times she had locked herself out. She
was always forgetting her key. Our front door opened onto
an open-air hallway, and I'd drive home early from work to
let her in so she wouldn't have to wait outside forever. She
worked in advertising, something to do with the European
market, so she went into work super early and got off in the
afternoon. "My rescuer!" she'd exclaim when I'd appear at
the top of the stairs. "Thank you, thank you, I'll buy you
booze!"

Phil and I slept together in my bed, which we'd done
countless nights before, but it felt different now without
Michelle across the hall.

"Move in with me," Phil whispered. I pretended I was
already asleep, because I wasn't sure what to say. I wasn't sure
what I wanted.

The next morning, Phil walked around naked, his
penis swinging everywhere. It was strange to see his penis
swinging around in my kitchen. He looked so carefree, like
this was normal, and maybe it was, maybe it would be the
new normal. Me and Phil, buying furniture and dancing past
midnight and putting up holiday decorations. Me and Phil,
walking around naked and fucking anywhere we wanted

because we didn't have to worry about a roommate walking in on us.

The blender was still in the corner where I'd thrown it, looking hurt and ugly, the cord flung out like a desperate drowning arm.

I realized, within the next few days, that my feelings for Michelle were deeper than I'd ever felt for Phil, and that I missed Michelle more than I'd ever missed Phil. Suddenly I felt sick that Phil and I had lasted this long, that I had let things get to this point. We were settled. Comfortable. It was perfectly normal for him to ask me to move in with him.

Two days later, when Phil picked me up for our Friday dinner date, I couldn't summon the enthusiasm to suggest a place. We ended up driving around aimlessly for a good twenty minutes before he finally swerved into the parking lot of Applebee's. "I could do with some riblets," he said, mimicking a Southern drawl, trying to make me laugh. I remember his earnest smile as he cut the engine and unbuckled his seatbelt, how carefree he looked in that moment. Riblets, beer, Friday night. Then he glanced over at me and his features drew in, his gaze sharpened. "What is it, Alina? Don't cry, baby. What's wrong?"

When Phil and I had been dating for three weeks – long enough that we felt relatively solid, that I still liked him, that he still called me – I felt comfortable telling my mother. I could hear her beaming over the phone. I shared the basics: grad student, Cal Tech, mechanical engineering, twenty-eight, never married, no kids.

"He sounds wonderful," she said, over and over. "Wonderful."

I couldn't remember the last time she'd sounded so proud. So relieved.

I've been home for only a couple minutes when my phone rings. "What is up with you?" Minnie asks, her tone accusing. She must be on her cell phone, leaving The Urth

Caffé. Wind cuts into her mouthpiece, drowning out her voice.

"What?" I say. "I can't hear you."

"Why'd you take off and leave me like that? You just disappeared."

"I told you, I had to use the bathroom."

"Yeah, but then you never came back."

I tell her that I did come back. "I saw you," I say. Now my tone is accusing. "I saw you with *her*."

"With Rachel? Why, do you know her or something?"

"Who's Rachel?"

"Craig's sister. She was eating a few tables over from us."

"Oh." I sit down on my red couch and hug a throw pillow to my chest. "No, I don't know her. I thought she was someone else."

"Who?"

"It doesn't matter. I'm sorry."

"Alina," Minnie says. Abruptly, the wind stops, and her voice sounds clear and close. "Michelle lives in London now, remember?"

"Yeah."

"And it wasn't about you. It didn't have anything to do with you. Sometimes people just need to move on. Life changes."

"Yeah."

"Are you okay? I worry about you."

"I'm fine," I say. "Don't worry. I'm fine."

"You're crazy!" Phil said that night in the Applebee's parking lot.

"I've seen the way you look at her."

"When am I even around her to look at her? It's not like she's ever at your place when I'm there."

"See! Suspicious. It's like the two of you are hiding something."

"Alina, really, you're being insane. I can't even remember the last time I saw Michelle. She's hardly been around at all the last few months."

I looked down at my lap, at my hands holding each other. "I don't love you," I said. "I'm sorry, but I don't."

So instead of moving in with Phil, I moved into a one-bedroom apartment on the other side of town, and I bought a bright red couch and casually mismatched pillows and a potted begonia for my windowsill. Sometimes at night, while watching TV, I look down at my hands, on my lap, holding each other.

The thing about living alone is, you have no one to double-check the locks. You climb into bed and turn off the light, and just then you hear a noise – a creak of the floorboards as the house resettles itself; the scratching of a tree branch against the windowpane. And you feel cold, and very alone, and you think of all those stories on the news about people living alone, young women especially, who get robbed or raped or murdered, and no one finds them for days and days, and you know it's old-fashioned to want a man to protect you, but really you just want someone, anyone, anyone else to climb out of bed and go check the deadbolt on the front door, to make sure it's bolted securely shut. But the thing about living alone is, there is no one else. There is only you. So you climb out of bed, hugging yourself against the chill, turning on lights in the bedroom, the hallway, the living room, the entryway, as you venture up to the front door, your own eyes shadowy hollows in the black pane of glass, and you see – there – relief – it's locked. You touch the deadbolt, you feel its weight beneath your fingers, just to be sure. It's locked, it's locked. You retreat back to your bedroom, turning off lights as you go, feeling better but still alone. And then you climb beneath the covers, pull them up to your chin, turn to one side, then the other, waiting for your body heat to warm them up, waiting, waiting.

Specks of Dust in Sunlight

Five days from now

Unable to sleep, Emily will dial the familiar ten digits and listen to the phone ring and ring and ring. When the message machine clicks on, it is not even his voice she hears, but her own. Or, not quite her own, either – it is the voice of her cheerful, skinny, high-school self, frozen on the machine's tape more than a dozen years ago. She hangs up, then dials again. It sickens her to hear the hollow ringing and ringing and then that voice, but once she's started dialing she can't seem to stop.

Yesterday

Emily had imagined the phone call would come in the empty early-morning hours – 3 a.m., 4 a.m. She thought some part of her would know before she even picked up the phone. *Gunny.* It would be her father on the other end, and she would listen to his words calmly, feeling numb. Or maybe the tears would come right away, engulfing her; maybe she wouldn't be able to get a single word out. Her father would be crying, too.

But the call comes in the middle of the afternoon – she is driving back to work after a long lunch break, during which she'd shoplifted a cheap plastic bracelet and three Milky Way bars from the convenience store after paying for her gas. She is eager to get back to work, park her car in the far space of the last row, and eat the three Milky Ways one after the other, her world narrowing to nothing but the almost painful sweetness of soft chocolate and caramel, the soothing crinkle of the torn-away wrappers.

She hears her phone ringing but her purse is out of reach, on the floor of the passenger's side, so she lets the call click over to voice-mail. After maneuvering into her far-away parking spot and pulling out her cell phone, she sees who called and doesn't bother listening to the message. Her mother always leaves long, rambling messages that the machine cuts off before she gets to the point of whatever it is she called about. Emily prefers to call back directly. And that's how she finds out.

"Fell all the way down the stairs," her mother explains. "We think it happened this morning. CeCe found him." CeCe is the woman who comes to clean Gunny's house once a week.

Emily twists the plastic bracelet around and around her wrist. She had imagined it would be the cancer returning, or a heart attack like Nana. Or a stroke. Or a slow sideways lolling into dementia. Not stairs.

"Your father seems to be holding up all right," her mother says. "But I thought it might be easier for him if I was the one who told you. Sweetheart? Are you still there?"

Emily promises to book a flight home for the funeral. She hangs up and sits in the silent bubble of her car, conscious of her own breathing. There are no tears. She doesn't feel numb, exactly. More than anything, it is a pressing need that fills her, like a buzzing weight on her chest. She rifles through her purse for the Milky Way bars and quickly unwraps them, one right after the other, and lines them up on the center console in neat row. *A Milky Way is a Milky Way is a Milky Way,* she thinks. *They are exactly like this, always.* The thought comforts her. She gulps them down in quick succession, licking the caramel from the corners of her mouth, and she feels better. She feels good enough to face the rest of the afternoon in her cubicle, trying to sell insurance to people who do not want to talk to her, who are already well enough aware of the dangers everyday life presents them without needing to hear it from her.

In a couple hours, her sugar-rush fades, replaced by a gnawing shame. At home, she folds the Milky Way wrappers into a tiny ball, which she crumples inside a napkin and stuffs at the bottom of the trash bin. Then she takes a walk to get away from her kitchen cupboards. Halfway down the block, she comes upon a girl drawing with chalk on the sidewalk, and she tries to give her the plastic bracelet but the girl shakes her head warily. "No thanks." In the morning, Emily's hollow stomach feels good, necessary, a physical venting of her guilt and grief. She does not eat anything for another day and a half, nothing but ice water and sugar-free gum.

Last year

Occasionally, when they say goodbye, Gunny calls her "Gail" by mistake. Emily doesn't correct him.

Three years ago

After the cancer diagnosis, Emily calls Gunny every night. They rarely talk more than a few minutes. Often Gunny repeats himself, as if his familiar stories and observations are worn grooves in a wooden tabletop, begging to be returned to again and again.

"I saw it was cold there today," he says, as he has said every night since Chicago's first snowfall in late November. "I looked it up in the paper this morning."

"Yep, it's pretty cold," Emily agrees. Or sometimes: "Yep, I miss California weather."

"You staying warm?" he asks, every night. "You've got good boots? A warm coat?"

"Yep, good and warm."

"How about gloves?"

"I've got warm gloves."

"Good," he says. "You stay warm now. You let me know if you need anything out there."

"I will," she tells him, though she doesn't think she could ever bring herself to ask him for money.

"You'll never guess where I went today," Gunny says.

"Where?"

"The mall."

She is surprised. Gunny has no patience for crowds. "Why'd you go there?"

"They had an advertisement about earmuffs in the paper," he says.

119

Emily sets down the stack of silverware she's been unloading from the dishwasher. *Oh, Gunny.* When she was home for Christmas, she stopped by his house most days to visit. They'd sit side-by-side on his brown leather couch, passing conversation idly back and forth, the TV blaring an old black-and-white Marx Brothers movie or a college basketball game. In one of these conversations, not thinking too much about it, Emily mentioned she'd looked for earmuffs in Chicago but hadn't found any she liked.

"But by the time I got down there," Gunny continues, "they were all gone. I was going to send them to you."

She thinks of him sitting on his couch, looking out the sliding glass door at the faraway ocean. She imagines the sunlight slanting into the room, revealing the dust on his coffee table and bookshelves. How strange that it's still daytime where he is, when it's already night for her. "Thanks, Gunny. But you don't need to get me earmuffs."

There is a pause.

"You don't need to worry about me," she adds.

"I'll keep looking," he says. "I'll find you some."

After she hangs up, the image persists – Gunny in his big boat of a car, with his enormous old man sunglasses, his mouth slightly open as it gets when he really concentrates. Him navigating the crowded mess of the parking lot, then slowly making his way through the buzzing metropolis of a department store, searching for the earmuffs she mentioned once, earmuffs to keep her warm, the newspaper advertisement fluttering in his hand, as he searches and searches but is unable to find them. Picturing it, her heart breaks and fills at the same time.

Four years ago

Emily uses her vacation time to go home, and sits with Gunny for the first week of his chemotherapy treatments. She expects him to look different somehow – gaunt, slack-jawed, scared. But he looks the same as ever. His face is clean-shaven, his jawline strong, and his eyes behind his round bifocals are clear, unclouded.

They sit there, quiet, watching the steady drip... drip... drip of the chemo into his veins. Emily is the first to tear her eyes away and claw at conversation. There is so much she has not told Gunny, so much he does not know about her life or the person she has become. To Gunny, she will always be a little girl in pigtail braids, or a teenager earnestly writing articles for the school newspaper, or a college student trying to make chocolate truffles at Christmas, tears of frustration welling in her eyes when they came out lumpy and burned. She is better, in Gunny's eyes, than she is anywhere else. She likes herself most when she is with him. Is that why she flew back to spend this week here, why she is sitting beside him in these stiff-backed hospital chairs, holding his jacket and massive wrap-around sunglasses on her lap? Is she doing this for Gunny, or for herself?

"Remember when you were four or five?" Gunny says suddenly, turning his face to look at her. The sunlight catches a patch of gray whiskers on his cheek that he must have missed shaving. "And your class went on a field trip to this hospital?"

Emily smiles and nods. It's been ages since she thought of this memory.

"Those elevator doors opened, and there you were!" Gunny says, clapping his hand on hers. "In all this great big hospital, your class was waiting for that exact elevator. Tell me, what were the chances of that?"

"Pretty slim."

"That's one of my favorite memories," he tells her. He settles back in his chair, glances at the IV attached to his arm, then out the window.

"Mine, too," Emily says, squeezing his hand.

Five years ago

Emily always calls Gunny on the anniversary of Nana's death, but this year she forgets. She has thrown

121

herself into work the past few months, skipping lunch and staying late; rumor has it a position in management is going to open up soon, and she's aiming for it. To be honest, though, she works to keep herself busy, away from the shell of her apartment. Before bed, she does hundreds of sit-ups, repeating positive mantras in her head: *Attitude is a little thing that makes a big difference. Every day may not be good, but there's something good in every day. If you don't like something change it; if you can't change it, change the way you think about it.* She fantasizes about running into David in a café, in their favorite bookstore, in the grocery store parking lot, and watching him do a double-take at her new thinness — *see my focus now, David, see my positive spirit, my energy?* — and begging her to take him back. In her fantasies, she always says no, but she knows in real life she would say yes. She would hate herself for it, but she would say yes.

She calls Gunny the next evening, watching a Lean Cuisine spin through the window of her microwave. Gunny's ancient phone makes his voice sound far away, as if he is speaking through a long empty tunnel.

"What?" Emily asks, pushing up the volume button on her headset as far as it will go. "I didn't catch that."

Gunny sighs. "I was just thinking, at least I was able to take her to those fancy restaurants those last years. She put up with a lot. She deserved it."

"You were busy," Emily says. "You had a busy practice. Nana understood that."

"No, I could have given her more of my time. I knew she was drinking too much and I just let it go. I should have taken better care of her."

"Oh, Gunny." Emily doesn't know what to say. Gunny has never been this open with her about Gail. "Nana knew you loved her."

Gunny is quiet. Or maybe Emily just can't hear him.

After a moment, she says, "I'm wearing her sweater today. The one with the pearl buttons. I get so many compliments whenever I wear it." This is a lie, but she knows

122

it will make Gunny happy. In reality, the sweater lives in the bottom drawer of her dresser, wedged under the ill-fitting pantyhose and padded bra she bought for David. She knows she'll never wear them again but they were so expensive she can't find the heart to throw them away.

A few days later, she pops into the pharmacy to pick up her birth control – each pill a reminder of the sex she isn't having – and, on the way out, she grabs a package of M&Ms, because it's a Friday and she's been good this week and they're a new flavor, coconut, and she's curious. She's already paid for her prescription, so she goes up to the front to pay for her candy, and there he is. David. His back is to her; he hasn't seen her yet. For all the fantasizing, she isn't ready. She remembers the last time she saw him, the click of the door closing as he left her standing there in the hallway, goosebumps rising on her arms underneath her thin coat. She pockets the M&Ms without paying and rushes outside, into her car, and away.

Six years ago

David breaks up with her because she isn't a happy enough person and her unhappiness is encroaching on his happiness and making him depressed. That's the phrasing he uses – "encroaching," as if she harbors some contagious disease. "You're always complaining about things," he says. "Your job, your weight, your mom."

"Don't bring my mother into this."

"I'm tired of living with your negativity all the time," David says. "It's exhausting."

"Just leave then!" Emily tells him, feeling like she is playing a part in some movie, the part where the two leads get into a huge fight and say things they don't mean. "If you're so unhappy, leave!"

David leaves. When she is at work the next day he comes back and cleans out all his things, plus a Blind Pilot CD she knows was hers not his. She does not call him, still feeling like she is playing a part in a movie, waiting for their inevitable apologetic reunion and incredible make-up sex. But it does not come. After a couple weeks she is telling herself, *At least you got to keep the apartment. It is a great apartment.*

Her mother calls often. "Why don't you move back home?" she says.

"I'm settled," Emily says. "I have a good job. My life is here."

Gunny doesn't broach the subject directly, but he calls her every couple of weeks and she can tell from his voice that he worries about her.

"Do you need anything?" he asks.

"No, I'm doing fine."

"Okay. Well, you'll let me know, right? If you need anything. I'm always here."

"Thanks, Gunny. I will."

The next week, she receives a check in the mail from him. She uses it to buy a new push-up bra and pantyhose, which she puts on and covers with only a trench coat. It is a twenty-minute ride on the El to David's new apartment. She huddles in her seat next to the window, looking out at the shadows of the city, freezing.

She can't tell from David's expression if he is surprised or unsurprised to see her. He steps aside to let her in; she closes the door behind her and slowly unbuttons her coat, trying to act like someone else, someone effortlessly sexy and comfortable with themselves. She remembers the night in college when David bent over her, kissing her stomach and thighs and the backs of her knees, a trail of kisses all the way down to her ankles and back up to her forehead, cheeks, lips. *I felt like Clare Danes in the Romeo & Juliet movie*, she'd confessed to her friend Diana, who'd laughed as if Emily was making a joke, but Emily had been serious. Now, David looks her up and down, draws in a deep breath, and shakes his head no. No, no, no. He moves to open the door, to usher her back outside into the night. She has never felt smaller.

Eight years ago

When Gunny learns that Emily is moving to Chicago with David after graduation, where she will experience "real winter" for the first time, he leads her upstairs to the spare bedroom and opens the cedar chest at the foot of the bed.

"Here," he says. "Take what you want."

The chest is filled with Nana's sweaters. Thick cable-knit turtlenecks; chunky wool cardigans; cashmere scoop necks.

"Take them," Gunny says. "Take them all. She'd want you to have them."

Emily brings the sweaters home in two ancient paper shopping bags from Macy's. In her room, she takes each sweater out of the bag, holds it up in the light. She brings the sweaters to her face and breathes in, but they smell like cedar chest, nothing more. Some of them have small holes where they've been eaten away by moths.

Gunny comes over for dinner and Emily is wearing one of the sweaters, coral pink with pearl buttons. When Gunny sees, he puts his palm to his chest and leaves it there for what feels like a long time. His expression makes Emily feel embarrassed and she has to look away. She stares instead at his hand – his large purple-veined hand, pressed to his chest, where his heart beats. She thinks of his heart, beating, beating, beating, until he draws her in and hugs her, longer and tighter than usual.

Ten years ago

"They're delicious," Gunny says when Emily ruins the Christmas truffles. "They taste just like the ones your Nana used to make."

Emily knows he is just being nice. They taste bitter, and the texture is wrong – all crumbly, like old Play-doh. Still, she forces them down, one after the next, trying to hide the evidence of her failure.

"It was so sweet of you to make these, Em," her mother says, unwrapping one from its paper cup, balancing her coffee mug on her knee.

"Tastes just like Gail's used to, don't you think?" Gunny says.

Emily doesn't remember much about the old Christmases, back when her grandmother was alive, but she's seen photographs. Her favorite is of the three of them, Nana, Gunny, and little Emmy wearing her fancy red Christmas dress with the white lace trim. Nana is bending down, squeezing Emmy's waist, and Gunny is standing in the background next to the white-flocked Christmas tree. He is not looking at the camera, he is looking at Nana and Emmy – his is a pure smile, caught in the moment.

"You used to call them Nana's little cupcakes," Gunny says to Emily. "You used to gobble them up."

Thirteen years ago

Emily comes home from her first semester of college feeling like her old life is a ratty, too-small sweater, like she is bursting its seams – her childhood bedroom feels like the set of a TV show, familiar yet foreign. Everything in her hometown is stale and small and far removed from her new, worldly, independent life. Gunny's house somehow is the only place that feels unchanged, maybe because it's always had a nostalgic atmosphere since Nana died. Artifacts still linger all around the house, filled with her presence. Gunny cuts two slices of banana bread and they sit and talk in the yellow-wallpapered kitchen.

"English, huh?" Gunny says about Emily's newly declared major. "You must get that from your grandmother."

"Really? Nana was an English major?" Emily wonders what her grandmother's favorite book was. Last semester in her American Lit class, Emily read the classics – Hemingway, Fitzgerald, Steinbeck – and now she imagines Nana's eyes passing over the same words, rereading passages like Emily had, completely taken in.

126

"Not exactly," Gunny says. "But she read all the time. That woman loved to read. Always had a thick book on the table there." He gestures to the other side of the breakfast nook, where an ancient cardboard box of Nana's sweetener packets still sits. Gunny drinks his coffee black.

"She was an English teacher," Gunny continues. "When I was in med school, in New York. I'd take the subway into the city to go to school, and she'd take the car and drive out to Hoboken to teach high school."

Emily adds this new nugget to her mental catalogue of information about the grandmother she barely remembers: *She wore red lipstick. She made her own pasta, rolling out the dough on a slab of marble in her kitchen. She was an English teacher.*

"In fact," Gunny says, pushing himself up from his chair. "C'mon upstairs. I have a surprise for you."

Emily follows him up the carpeted stairs. He grips the railing tight and apologizes for going so slow. "It's these arthritic knees," he says, grimacing.

"It's okay," Emily says.

Gunny leads her into his old study, sunlight peeking through gaps in the decrepit wooden blinds, revealing dust. From a corner of the room, under a stack of old newspapers, he pulls out a large cardboard box.

"Your grandmother's," he tells her. "I thought you might want to have them."

Emily lifts up the flap, hands shaking.

Bright covers and flirtatious, gaudy fonts stare up at her. *Lord of Scoundrels. It Had to Be You. Flowers From the Storm. The Bride.*

"Wow," she says, stomach dropping in disappointment.

"That should keep you busy for a while!" Gunny says, beaming.

Emily nods. She closes the box and carries it out to her car. "Thank you," she says, hoping he doesn't notice the forced edges of her smile. "I can't wait to read them."

She drives around with the box in her trunk for three weeks, and then, right before she heads back to school for the spring semester, she drops by Goodwill. No one is working the front desk, so she sets the box down on the counter and leaves. She is in a rush, running late to meet her friend Katie for coffee.

Fifteen years ago

Gunny asks her to record the message on his answering machine. "No one wants to hear the voice of an old guy like me," he says.

"But it's your house," Emily says. "Won't it be confusing when people call?"

"The people who matter won't be confused – they know who you are. I'm tired of listening to my own voice when I check my messages."

"Okay," Emily says slowly, watching as Gunny unwinds the tape in the machine. "What do you want me to say?"

"Oh, you know, whatever comes to mind," Gunny says. "Ready?"

He presses the button and the machine beeps. Emily leans down close to the microphone. "Hi," she says. "You've reached Gunny. He's not home right now, so please leave a message. He'll get back to you as soon as he can…unless he accidentally deletes your message. Bye!"

Gunny laughs and hugs her. "That's my girl!" he says. "That was perfect."

Eighteen years ago

In his dresser drawer, Gunny has a stack of black-and-white snapshots of Gail at the beach.

"No, it's not the beach," he corrects Emily. "It's Muzzy's. That's the lake where I lifeguarded in the summertime."

"Oh," she says, feeling their weight in her hands – thick paper, almost cardboard. In the photos, Nana's skin is

128

tan and smooth. She's wearing a dark one-piece bathing suit and her hair is cropped short in a pageboy style.

"She was breathtaking, your grandma," Gunny says. He touches the edge of the photo lightly with his fingertips.

Emily murmurs agreement, wishing she could remember Nana better. She wants to grow up to be just like her. Beautiful, stylish, smart, happy. The perfect mother. The perfect wife. Emily wonders if, when she grows up, she will ever find someone who loves her as much as Gunny loved Gail. Somehow, it doesn't seem likely.

Twenty-two years ago

This Christmas, the Christmas after Nana died, Emily's parents host dinner at their house. They invite Gunny, and Nana's brother and his family, and Emily's uncles and aunts and cousins on her mom's side. The house feels hot and small. The kitchen and dining room have never held so many people and the wooden floors groan more than usual, as if protesting.

When Nana was alive, she would host Christmas dinner. During present-unwrapping time, Gunny would always sit on a chair off to the side. When Emily found a gift under the tree with his name on it, she would bring it to him and he would say, "For me? Thank you!" as if she were delivering a million-dollar game-show prize.

This year, she is the one who brings him the flat, square box. She stands beside him as he opens it, looking over his shoulder. It is a black-and-white photo of a young man and a young woman wearing bathing suits. She doesn't recognize either of the people in the photo.

Suddenly, it seems like she and Gunny are in a play that all the grown-ups are watching. Emily can sense their hushed breath.

"Oh," one of them says. "Oh my goodness."

Then Emily realizes Gunny is crying. That isn't what is supposed to happen. What happens is, she brings Gunny a present, and he smiles and gives her a hug and opens it and says, "Oh, how nice!" or "I've been wanting this!" in his big-people voice, and she feels proud for bringing it to him. Now, she feels responsible for his crying. She hugs him, and he hugs her back, but he is breathing unevenly, scary shaky breaths lodged with tears.

Later, Emily's mother explains to her that the people in the photo were Gunny and Nana, a long time ago. Emily doesn't quite believe her.

Twenty-five years ago

Emily's kindergarten class takes a trip to the hospital. Years later, she will not remember walking in a single-file line past the nursery and peering in at the newborn babies swaddled in pink and blue; or the cups of strawberry Jello they eat for snack-time in the pediatric unit, stenciled drawings of Mickey and Minnie grinning down from the walls; or the refrigerator magnet boxes of Band-Aids they are given as souvenirs. What she will remember, the one image that crystallizes and holds in her mind, is this:

She is standing with her classmates, waiting for the light above the elevator to ding, for the doors to open and the elevator to take them back down to the lobby. Emily is a shy child, often nervous, easily frightened. She is ready for this field trip to be over, for them to leave the hospital and board the bus back to school. She is ready for her dad to pick her up in his rumbling white pickup and take her home. She is ready to be in her own safe room, with the painted blue walls and the drawing she made of ballerina shoes and her Barbie beach house. Emily shifts from foot to foot. Her stomach is an anxious twisting balloon animal.

The elevator doors open, and there stands Gunny. He is wearing his green surgical scrubs, the green cap pushed up on his head, covering his bald spot. But Emily recognizes him immediately. Her stomach settles itself, unclenching like a fist after a fight has been avoided.

He sees her at the same time she sees him.

Emily runs forward and throws herself in his arms. Gunny laughs and hugs her. He rubs her back with his hand.

"It's my Emmy!" he says. "It's my girl!"

She feels too happy to say anything. She grips his sleeve tightly in her fingers. She knows that in a few moments Gunny will put her down and she will have to let go of his sleeve and continue onto the elevator with the rest of her class, but she doesn't want to. She doesn't want to ever let go.

Hearts Like Lemons in Fists of Dew

June in Ventura is a gloomy month. The fog creeps in from the ocean and stretches its fingers inland, settling in the creases of the hills, the spaces between office buildings, the narrow yards of houses. Cars maneuver slowly down Foothill Road, their headlights on even in the middle of the afternoon. The fog makes seeing difficult. It seeps down Main Street, covering the shops and restaurants so only the heads of the palm trees and the arching buttresses of the movie theater stretch above it, peering over the fog like tall people peer over a crowd. At Poinsettia Elementary School, in these last days before summer, recess becomes a giant game of hide-and-seek, children slinking through the fog-covered soccer fields, refusing to come back inside when the bell rings. The fog sinks down over the lemon orchards like a thick blanket, catching in the branches of trees and wrapping the small, unripened lemons in fists of dew.

The air is chilly and damp. Sweater weather.

A heavy midmorning lethargy persists throughout the day. But at night, the fog lifts, and people go outside in their backyards and driveways to gaze at the stars in the crisp, clear sky. At bedtime, anticipation flutters across the city. People close their eyes, hoping to wake up and find morning sunshine, warmth, summer.

Michelle returns to Ventura on a foggy day. She'd forgotten how, in the fog, even the most familiar streets seem cloaked in secrets. The entire town feels quiet, under siege.

She turns into the driveway of her house – her parents' house, the house she grew up in – and cuts the engine. The blinds are slanted closed, all the way closed, even in the upstairs bedroom windows. The rosebushes have been recently pruned, beaten back to thorny stumps, and the jacaranda tree that Michelle and Rae climbed as children has been uprooted. *Diseased,* Michelle's mother told her over the phone. Michelle tried to prepare herself for its absence, but she is shaken to see the tree gone. Even the stump has been removed, and the spot where it used to be is now patched over with sod. Without the jacaranda tree, her parents' house looks naked, vulnerable. Like a ship that has battened down the hatches, floating unanchored in a roiling sea of fog.

When Michelle was fifteen, Rae's family moved away. Michelle sobbed in the bathroom, her cheek pressed against the cool tile. Her mother came in with freshly laundered towels and found her lying there.

"Honey, oh baby," her mother said, coaxing Michelle off the floor and onto her bed, stroking her hair.

"I loved her," Michelle sobbed. "I loved her so much."

"I know you did."

"No, I mean I *loved* her, Mom. I still am in love with her."

Her mother smoothed Michelle's hair away from her forehead. "Oh, honey. You don't know what love is. This is called grieving."

"She was my soul mate," Michelle said.

"Dr. Lassen says it's normal for you to feel this way." Her mother reached over and plucked a tissue from the box on the nightstand. "Shelly, listen to me. You're a strong girl," she said. "You're going to be okay. Someday this will all feel like a long time ago."

Michelle climbs out of her car and stretches. The fog is so thick that Rae's old house across the street is just a shadow, like the beginnings of an idea before it is fully formed.

On summer mornings like this, she and Rae would escape into the fog after breakfast and race down the block, across El Dorado Street and into the lemon orchard. Their favorite tree was an old, gnarled beauty seven rows up, far enough from El Dorado that traffic noise didn't reach them. The lemon orchard was their place, their Shell and Rae Hideaway, and on foggy days its mystery was amplified, its

133

solitude more pronounced. On foggy days, anything could happen.

Rae disappeared on a foggy day.

"In here," Michelle's mother calls from the depths of the house. Michelle shuts the front door behind her and abandons her duffel bag in the entryway. With all the blinds shut, the living room is dim, but a light blazes from the kitchen. She finds her mother elbows-deep in a bowl of ground meat. She smiles at Michelle and wipes a strand of hair across her forehead with the inside of her wrist.

"Well, if it isn't my world traveler," she says. Michelle moves in to hug her, but her mother steps back, studying her daughter's face. "Look at you," she announces after a few moments. "You look great."

"Thanks, Mom. You too."

"You look healthy. I'm glad. I'm always worried you'll come back all bones. Supposed to be the food in England's terrible."

"It's not so bad," Michelle says.

"Well, I hope you're not too cultured for your mom's meatloaf, because that's what I'm making tonight."

"No, that sounds great."

"Your father requested it. And used to be you loved my meatloaf."

"I still do."

"You would have eaten it every night if you could."

Michelle smiles, but the skin on her face feels tight. "Nothing beats your cooking, Mom."

"That's what a mother likes to hear." She washes her hands in the kitchen sink and flicks them dry. Michelle glances around the kitchen. It looks the same – paisley patterned wallpaper, ceramic sunflower cookie jar, hand-painted plates displayed above the breakfast nook. But it seems smaller than the kitchen of her childhood. Across the room, still proudly taped to the refrigerator door, is the rainbow of ribbons Michelle won in youth track meets.

Her mother holds out her arms. "Come give me a hug."

Michelle is a good three inches taller than her mother, and she hunches around her like a shell, as if shielding her from something dangerous. Her mother's hair smells the same, a faint whiff of coconut shampoo and the hot metal of her straightening iron. After only a few moments, her mother disengages herself and turns back to the bowl of bloody meat. "Gotta get this in the oven," she says. Then, her tone casual: "Your father's upstairs, if you want to say hi."

That summer, Rae's face smiled from MISSING posters throughout the city. Michelle taped the posters to lampposts and slipped them under windshield wipers and stuffed them into mailboxes. *If I give her photograph to every single person in town, then she will come home and everything will be Okay.*

But Rae stayed missing.

Authorities combed the lemon orchard, but found nothing. Not a charm from her bracelet. Not a pink shoelace. Not a single strand of her dark hair.

A suspect was never named.

A funeral was never held.

That winter, Rae's family moved away. Michelle never set foot in the orchard again.

When Michelle's parents bought this house, it was freshly built in a just-opened housing development. Michelle was a little over a year old. She doesn't remember living anywhere else, doesn't remember the fresh-paint, new-carpet smell of the big empty rooms. She has seen pictures, snapped on a disposable camera, of the house when it was brand new – vulnerable flowerbeds, the jacaranda tree just a sapling, braced with wooden stakes. Michelle cannot remember the tree as anything less than magnificent, its purple-blossomed branches stretching towards the sky, perfect for climbing. She wonders, if the tree were still there, if it would seem smaller too.

Rae's family moved in across the street when Michelle was three. One of her earliest memories is sitting in a little red wagon with Rae, being pulled along the sidewalk by Rae's older brother Jonathan. Rae had shiny dark hair and a moon-shaped birthmark on her right knee. She wore a silver charm bracelet and bright pink tennis shoes. She liked holding Michelle's hand, and her hands were always cool and dry. Even as they grew older, even as they stopped holding their parents' hands to cross the street, Rae would still grab Michelle's hand when she was excited. As if she were trying to transfer emotion from her palm to Michelle's.

As kids, they shared every shivery detail of their lives. Rae's distrust of the ice-cream man. Michelle's dream of drowning. Rae's love of lime-green Skittles. Michelle's fear of snails. They were born one year and one month apart, and Michelle often daydreamed that Rae was her sister, and that she, Michelle, had been given to her parents because Rae's family already had Jonathan and Rae, and Michelle's parents didn't have anyone. Once upon a time they'd had another daughter – Laura – but she had died before Michelle was born. Her parents only spoke about her once, when Michelle had to bring in a baby photo for her fifth-grade yearbook and found a photo of baby Laura wedged in the front of an old photo album.

Michelle's hair sprang up in tufted golden curls, and her compact frame was the opposite of Rae's willowy height. But they had the same sun-freckled shoulders, and Michelle liked to imagine the same blood flowed through their veins. Until the foggy June Michelle turned fourteen, and suddenly Rae didn't feel like a sister anymore. Inkling feelings, leaking out, expanding. Like an overripe lemon, skin stretched taught with pulp and juice, ready to drop from the tree.

Upstairs in the master bedroom, Michelle's father is propped up with pillows in the king-sized bed, dozing in front of the T.V. where Anderson Cooper broadcasts live from the Gulf Oil Crisis. The volume is turned down so low that his voice is an unintelligible murmur. Michelle hovers in the doorway. Her father looks much older than his sixty years – painfully frail, his cheeks sunken, a blanket pulled all the way up to his chin. Michelle tries to summon the memory of her father in the green windbreaker and bright yellow baseball cap, tries to reconcile that man with the withered man dozing before her. Despair wells up in her throat. She lets her eyes wander to the glowing T.V. screen, the images of the wounded ocean bleeding oil.

"A shame, isn't it?" Michelle's father peers at the television. "A damn shame," he repeats, shaking his head.

"The news is always depressing," Michelle says, searching through the layers of blankets for the remote control. "You should be watching something else. Don't they play M*A*S*H reruns on one of these channels? Or there's probably a game on somewhere."

"I don't want to watch television," her father says, nodding towards the bedside chair. "I want to talk to my daughter. You look beautiful. When did you get in?"

Michelle sits, hugging her belly. "Just now. Traffic was horrible on the 101."

"But you made it safe. That's what matters. It's good to see you."

"You too, Dad." Michelle can't hold her father's gaze for long, so she reaches for his hand and holds that instead. His hand is a cold potato with shriveled skin. Instinctively, Michelle glances towards the window, but the blinds are shut tight.

That June day, the day everything changed, Michelle ran upstairs to her room and vomited once more into the toilet. She leaned against the sink, swishing mouthwash around and around her teeth. It stung her gums. She kept swishing. Finally, she spit it out. She spit it out and kept spitting, fiercely, rhythmically. Her eyes squeezed shut, as if in prayer.

"So how's work treating you?" Michelle's father asks.

"Fine," Michelle says. "You know – busy as always." It's true – the London advertising firm she works for is one of the top in Europe.

"Any opportunities for a transfer coming up, you think?"

"Dad, please – "

"I'm just asking. I thought you said you'd think about it."

"I really don't want to get into this now."

Her father draws his hand away from Michelle's and coughs weakly into his fist. He wipes his mouth with a crumpled tissue. "I worry about your mother, after all this is over."

"Don't say it like that."

"I'm just telling it like it is. I know your mother. She hates to be alone."

"Mom? She's never struck me that way."

"She's more fragile than she lets on. She misses you. London is so far away, Shelly. Why do you have to be so far away?"

"It's not that far. All I have to do is hop on a plane and I'm here."

"There must be great advertising jobs in Los Angeles."

"I like London. I'm happy there."

Her father's hand clenches and unclenches a fold of blanket. "I don't know what we did wrong. You couldn't wait to put an entire continent and an ocean between us."

"Dad, it's not like that." Michelle reaches for his hand again. "I'll think about it, okay?"

On the TV screen, a young man smiles to show his gleaming white teeth, free of coffee stains, and holds up a new brand of toothpaste. The commercials are always louder than the TV programs, and the toothpaste jingle fills the darkened room like a gust of wind. Michelle wants to crawl into the commercial and live there. She would marry the smiling man and floss every day and spend the rest of her life under safe fluorescent lighting.

"I should let you rest," Michelle says, releasing her father's hand and standing up. "I'll come get you when dinner's ready."

Her father opens his mouth as if to say something, but then only nods and lets his head fall back against the pillows.

Michelle began running track after Rae's family moved away. She ran the mile and the two-mile. She developed a habit of vomiting after races. Her coach said she pushed herself too hard.

Michelle's father attended all her track meets. He was a firm believer in positive reinforcement and parental support, vowing to be different than his own parents, who had never attended a single one of his boyhood tennis matches or football games.

Michelle's mother defended her in-laws. "They had five kids to worry about. We only have Michelle."

Still, there were a lot of track meets, and her father did not miss a single one. He'd settle himself in the top row of the rickety wooden bleachers, wearing his green windbreaker and bright yellow baseball cap, giving Michelle a thumb's up as she nervously jogged to the starting line before a race. There was something fierce and protective in her father's devotion to her track meets, as if he was trying to ward off ever-lurking danger, control what was uncontrollable. *If I cheer on my daughter at every single track meet, I will be a Good Father and she will turn out Okay.* Driving home after the meets, Michelle's father would put on his *Best of James Taylor* CD. Sometimes Michelle felt like talking about the race, and her father turned the volume down. Other times Michelle gazed out the window, silent and spent, and the only voice in the car was James' crooning.

"I would always glance at the stands, hoping to see my parents," Michelle's father confessed once at the dinner table. "It would have been great to see them there. To know they were proud of me."

"Of course they were proud of you," Michelle's mother said. "It was a different time then. People didn't say 'I love you.' They didn't need to. You just know love."

Afterwards, Michelle vomited into a clutch of leaves while Jonathan looked away. He asked if she was okay. He asked her not to tell anyone.

"I think it'll be best if this is our secret," he said. Michelle nodded, standing up. Her legs felt hollow.

"Rae's not in my room," she said. "I was being honest."

"I'm sure she's at our house then. We probably missed her somehow."

As they left the orchard, the fog was clearing. Michelle searched for the moon, but it was a new moon, only a tiny sliver of light in the darkness.

"It's not like your father has the flu," Michelle's mother says, wrenching the knife into the meatloaf. She cuts a thick slice, which she spatulas onto a plate. "He's not getting better, honey."

"I know that."

"We eat dinner in the bedroom now. He doesn't have the strength to go up and down those stairs."

Michelle grabs a tumbler from the cupboard above the sink and fills it with water from the tap. The same tumblers from her childhood, made of gauzy blue glass. Rae once called them mermaid cups, as if the ocean had been frozen into dishware, the ideal ocean blue of animated movies and coloring books. Different from the real ocean ten minutes away, closer to brown than blue and flecked with seaweed and tasting bitter, acrid – not the way water was supposed to taste.

"No, dear – use the Britta," her mother scolds. "The tap water isn't good here, remember?"

Michelle pretends not to hear, downing the glass, remembering the sting of ocean water up her nose, the sour vinegar of it in her mouth, spitting it out and spitting again and again and again, trying to dislodge the taste.

That June evening, Michelle led Jonathan through the orchard, exhilarated anger fizzing inside her, picturing the shock that would fill Rae's face upon seeing her brother in their hideaway. She wanted to see hurt in Rae's eyes. She wanted to show Rae that it didn't matter, none of it – all their whispered confessions, their jokes, their promises – it was all just childhood stuff. Silly games. Pretending.

Michelle didn't know she was going to kiss Jonathan until they reached the old gnarled lemon tree and found it empty. Unease clenched her belly, but she told herself Rae was nearby. The next tree over. Watching.

"It's so dark here," Michelle said. And it was. The trees were shadowy figures with outstretched arms.

"Is this the one?" Jonathan asked, nudging his foot against the lemon tree.

"Yep. This is our hideout."

"Rae?" Jonathan called. "Rae!"

"Rae!" Michelle yelled.

Somewhere in the distance, an owl hooted.

Michelle stepped closer to Jonathan. "It's spooky in here," she said, hugging her arms.

Jonathan looked down at her, and something shifted in his expression. "You scared?" he said, putting an arm around her. His arm was heavy and his arm-hair prickled Michelle's bare back.

Michelle nodded and bit her lip. She *was* scared, suddenly. She and Rae had never ventured into the orchard after dark. Everything felt heightened. The rustling of the leaves, the shadowed trunks of the trees were like something out of a dream, a fever-dream, disorienting. Like when she conjured a place in her dreams and it was different from the real place.

"Don't be scared," Jonathan said, tightening his arm around her. There was something in his voice that Michelle had never heard there before. She knew what was going to happen and she imagined Rae was hiding nearby, watching. Defiantly, Michelle tilted her face up to his.

It was not what she expected. It was not sweet or gentle. His beard was rough against her face. He pressed her against the tree and Michelle felt her fear expand until it filled her completely.

"What about Rae?" she said. "We should find Rae."

Jonathan grinned at her. "You and I both know why you brought me here, and it wasn't to find Rae. She's upstairs in your room right now." He leaned closer. He smelled of sweat and cigarette smoke. "I could always tell you had a thing for me."

On foggy days, anything could happen.

It was Rae she thought about as he held her to him there, his hands pulling at her hair. She thought of Rae and she felt angry and panicky, like the order of the world had fallen away, and she knew it was her fault. She was the one who had started it all. She had blurred the line between them, and then she had left Rae there alone. Michelle knelt in the dirt of the orchard, at the base of their lemon tree. She kept her eyes closed. She fought the impulse to gag. She offered this as her penance.

Then, the taste of the ocean, bitter and acrid. Jonathan released her and she spit it out and spit again and again and again, trying to dislodge the taste.

"This tastes delicious, Evelyn," Michelle's father says, a napkin tucked under his chin. He used to be a fast eater, sometimes even burning his mouth because of his impatience to fill his stomach. Now his chewing is delicate and painful.

Her mother smiles. "I'm glad you like it, Frank."

"Yeah, Mom, this is great," Michelle chimes in, feeling like she missed her cue. "It's good to be home."

Her mother raises an eyebrow. "I'm surprised to hear you call this home."

"Evelyn – "

"What I mean is, I'm glad to hear her say it. I'm *glad* to hear you say it, Michelle. I just thought maybe you'd outgrown this place."

"Well, yeah, I grew up. But this house will always be home."

Michelle catches a glance between her parents and the knowledge hits her. Still, she asks: "What? What was that look?"

"Nothing," her mother says.

"Tell me."

Michelle's father sighs. "We're selling the house, sweetheart."

"When?"

"We had our first meeting with the realtor last week."

"Where will you live?"

"I'll just get a nice little apartment in town," her mother says. "Or a condo. It doesn't make sense to keep this place. It's too big."

Michelle nods and takes a bite of meatloaf. Her mouth is dry. The meatloaf is hard to swallow. She chews and chews. Her father chews, her mother chews. The dim room is filled with their chewing.

That June day, Michelle hadn't wanted to answer the door. She thought it was Rae, wanting to apologize, to explain, to talk. She couldn't handle seeing Rae. Not for a while.

But the knocking persisted, so Michelle undid the latch and yanked the door open. Rae's brother Jonathan stood on the front porch. Behind him, the sun sank blearily through the fog. Jonathan was sixteen, with Rae's dark hair but a thicker build and curling, sarcastic lips. He was growing a beard and it shadowed his jowls in patches.

"Rae's supposed to come home. It's time for dinner," he said.

"She's not here."

"She's not?"

Michelle shrugged. "Sorry. I don't know where she is."

"Bullshit, you two are attached at the hip. I know she's hiding in your room or something. It's her night to do the dishes and I'm not letting her push it off on me again."

"We were hanging out earlier, but then I had to leave. You can search my room if you want. She's not there."

"Well, she hasn't come home," Jonathan said. "It'll be dark soon. You know better than me where she could be."

Michelle and Rae were eight years old when they first ventured into the orchard and claimed the gnarled lemon tree as their hideaway. "I have an idea," Rae had said. "Let's promise never to show this place to anyone. It's our secret." Michelle promised. Rae stole a paring knife from her family's cutlery drawer and they carved their names into the tree trunk.

"I think I know where she is," Michelle told Jonathan. She hollered to her parents that she was going over to Rae's for dinner, then stepped outside and closed the door behind her. "C'mon, I'll show you."

Michelle kisses her father goodnight and helps her mother with the dishes. She reclines on the living room couch and tries to read, but can't focus. Her mother rifles through stacks of junk mail on the end table.

"Have you seen my reading glasses, Shelly?"

"No. Sorry."

"This is what happens when you get old. You start losing things."

"We all lose things."

"Please don't take that tone with me, Michelle. Please don't start."

"I'm sorry, it's just – I can't believe you're selling the house. Is it because of finances? I can send more money if that's the reason – "

"No, it's not. Your father and I are managing just fine. Thank God the firm gave him good health insurance."

"Then why are you selling it?"

"Like I said before, it's too big. Too big and too empty."

"Maybe if you opened the blinds it wouldn't feel like such a morgue in here."

"And look out the window at what? The fog? You can hardly see across the yard. It makes you father anxious, and I don't much care for it either."

"C'mon, Mom. I know how much you love this house."

"Love changes. Now I just want a fresh start, away from all these memories."

"You say that like you hate it here."

"Michelle, listen to yourself. It's not fair for you to act like you suddenly care about this place."

"This is my home too."

"You've visited three times in eight years. The only reason I could get you home now is because of your father."

Michelle stands up, feeling claustrophobic. "I've missed it here, actually." She crosses the room and takes a jacket from the hall closet.

"Where are you going?" her mother asks.

"Just out for a short walk."

"It's dark out. Be careful."

"I will," Michelle says, stepping outside into the night.

Michelle knew as soon as Rae pulled away. She wasn't smiling. Shame lurked in her eyes. She untangled her hand from Michelle's and wiped her mouth, the charms on her bracelet clinking softly against each other. Neither of them spoke. Michelle's hands shook as she swung herself down from the tree. Leaves littered the ground. She ran.

Rae called after her, tears in her voice: "You're my best friend!"

Michelle kept running.

It is a clear night, cool and quiet. Michelle breathes deeply. She heads out in the opposite direction from the orchard, but soon doubles back, feeling drawn towards the darkened trees.

She counts seven rows up and plunges in, heart racing, the dirt packed hard under her feet. The trees do seem smaller, the gaps between their branches wider than she remembers. Or maybe there is more moonlight tonight. Once, she stumbles over a root, but she catches herself before she falls.

She slows down, examining each tree, knowing she is close.

For the first time in years, she tries to summon Rae's face. She can picture her dark hair, she can hear her laugh, but her features have become a blur.

The trees all look the same. Michelle thought some part of her would *know* when she found their tree, but now she's not so sure. It's been years. The tree was old. Maybe it died. Maybe it was yanked out and a new tree was planted where it used to be.

Michelle hoists herself up onto a branch. She sits there for a long time, swinging her legs in the dark. She expected Rae to be everywhere in this orchard, but this orchard is not their orchard anymore. This tree is not their tree. Or maybe it is. She has no way of knowing.

Rae's lips were chapped. Her tongue tasted of bubblegum toothpaste.

When Michelle returns home, her mother is still awake, reading a magazine in the deep-seated armchair that used to be her father's favorite sitting place. Her small frame is swallowed up by the overstuffed cushions. The house looms around her, dark and cavernous.

"Mom," Michelle says, switching on another lamp. "Remember that day, a long time ago, when I told you I was in love with Rae?"

That June day, Rae and Michelle perched side-by-side on a branch of their lemon tree. The fog curled around them. Rae's hair glistened darkly in the shadows. Her bare shoulder leaned against Michelle's, a warm steady weight. Their legs dangled, their thighs touched. The moon-shaped birthmark on Rae's knee winked up at Michelle, as if it knew her secret.

Rae whistled a few notes. "Is that how the song goes?"

"What song?"

"That one we heard on the radio. I can't remember the words."

"I don't know," Michelle said.

Rae whistled the notes again. Her voice sounded loud in the stillness of the orchard. Then, abruptly, she stopped, turning to Michelle with wide eyes.

"Did you hear that?" she whispered.

"What?"

"I swear I just heard a footstep."

"I didn't hear anything."

"Someone's out there," Rae said. She nestled her body closer to Michelle's. Beneath them, the tree branch shifted. A lemon fell and thumped softly on the ground.

"There," Rae said. "What was that?"

Michelle laughed. "It was a lemon. You're such a dork."

"I think someone's out there." Rae reached for Michelle's hand.

The dark leaves whispered to each other. The fog pressed close.

Michelle met Rae's eyes. She leaned in, lips parted, knowing that nothing would ever be the same.

147

Under the Jacaranda Trees

It is a gray-skied afternoon in June, the clouds pressing down around the purple hills, when Kate calls and invites me over for a picnic.

"Not my house, actually," she clarifies. "Jay's having people over. Did you know he has a pizza oven in his backyard?"

Jay is Kate's boyfriend. I've only met him once. Kate and I are new friends – we met last month in yoga class – but I can already feel myself relaxing into a trusting, intimate closeness. It feels like Kate strode into that yoga studio, plunked her purse down next to my bag, unfurled her mat next to mine, and chose me. She's probably one of those people who everyone feels close to – she's always sharing her food with you across the table, touching your back or your wrist as she tells a story, introducing you to people with a wide, genuine smile. Around her, I sometimes feel stiff and awkward, a puppet-person, but it's an awkwardness suffused with gratitude.

"Come over," she says now. "We're making pizzas. The dogs are all running around."

Kate has two dogs and Jay has two more. That's how they met – at doggy obedience class. My friend Bee calls stories like that "meet-cutes." I've never in my life had a meet-cute. I can't even remember how I met half the men I've dated. The other half I met over sloshed drinks in cheap bars.

I tell Kate I'll be over soon.

"Yay, can't wait to see you!" she says. My heart leaps – *I'm wanted! I'm loved!* – even though I know it's just Kate being Kate.

Jay lives in a small ranch-style house at the end of a cul-de-sac, jacaranda trees raining purple flowers over the front lawn and driveway. I park across the street. The fog presses in close. I lock up and cross to the house, wishing I'd worn a sweater instead of a thin T-shirt. Rifling through my

148

closet for appropriate outerwear had seemed too much effort; it was all I could do to gather my keys and wallet and get out the door. This weather makes time compress and expand, so my Sunday-morning lethargy lasts all afternoon. Soon the sun will plunge behind the hills and night will settle over everything.

I ring the doorbell. No one answers. The bottle of wine I picked up on the way over feels damp in my hand. I consider turning around and retreating, but my cell phone buzzes in my pocket. A message from Kate: *We're in the backyard. Just come around back when you get here. xoxo!*

I step through the grass to the side of the house and reach over the wooden gate, fumbling with the latch; when I try to push it open with my hip, it won't budge. This is why I hate socializing. So many tests to pass. I give the gate one more shove with my foot and this time it opens, banging loudly against a trashcan. Within seconds, I'm surrounded by a mass of yapping terriers, collars jingling daintily, a blur of gray and white. There's also a beautiful golden retriever that jumps up, paws batting my chest. I pet its head, jam my phone back into my pocket, and hold the wine aloft like a trophy.

"Blue! Down!" a man calls, jogging towards us. He grabs the retriever's collar and pulls the dog away. "Sorry about that. Blue knows not to jump, but sometimes she gets excited around new people and can't help herself." The man has kind brown eyes and a small mole on one cheek. "I'm Scott," he says, reaching out a hand.

I wipe my palm on my jeans and enclose my fingers around his. "Deepti," I say.

"That's a pretty name," he says.

"Thank you."

The dogs scuffle around our feet. He shakes my hand for longer than I'm used to. It feels intimate, something I never thought a handshake could be.

"Deepti! You found us!" Kate exclaims, sweeping into the side yard. She wears her dark curly hair in a great pile

149

on top of her head, kept aloft with bobby pins and butterfly clips. Scott releases my hand. Kate gently shoos the dogs away with her bare feet. "Ooh, you brought wine!" She accepts the bottle and guides me, a hand at my back, into the backyard. The first thing I notice is the pizza oven, a tower of brick and stone with a gaping oven mouth. It's much bigger than I expected. Around the oven is an outdoor kitchen space: smooth granite counters, sink, mini-fridge. The yard is ringed with more jacaranda trees, fallen purple blossoms littering the grass and patio like confetti. The dogs chase each other in circles around the outdoor fire pit.

"Everyone, this is Deepti!" Kate announces, her voice full of pride, as if I'm some rare treasure she's stumbled across. She hands the wine to Jay and leads me around, making introductions. "This is John and Eleanor, they live down in L.A. – Eleanor and I met through work. She's an actress! Over there talking to Jay, that's Todd, and his boyfriend Bryan is here somewhere too, he must be inside – you'll meet him in a minute."

"He's in the kitchen making brownies!" Eleanor interjects, leaning across John's lap to wink at Kate. "He makes the *best* brownies," she says to me.

I feel suddenly nervous. Is she hinting at pot brownies? The last time I had pot brownies, the night did not end well.

Kate is not finished with introductions. "And this, Deepti," she continues, her hand on my elbow, and she guides me around the counter to where an old woman in a fleece jacket sits on a stool, chopping cilantro. She wears a multicolored knit cap pulled down over her ears, her white hair tufting out the back and sides like cotton batting. "This is Mama Lucy, Jay's mom."

"It's nice to meet you," I say.

"Now what do you do?" Mama Lucy says, not looking up from her cutting board.

"Oh, um, I do marketing for JuJu Water – maybe you've heard of us?"

Mama Lucy frowns. One of the biggest problems I'm facing in my new job is that nobody knows us. In marketing, there's a principle called the mere-exposure effect, which means people tend to prefer products they're familiar with. So to convince someone to buy your product, you've got to outdo their bias for more-familiar brands. It's not just true in marketing. The mere-exposure effect is one of the reasons it took me so long to break up with Phil.

Kate steps in. "JuJu Water – remember, Mama Lucy, we brought you that coconut orange juice that time? That's the company Deepti works for."

Mama Lucy nods absently. Bits of cilantro cling to the blade.

"Deepti's terrific at her job," Kate continues. "They brought her out here from New York City!"

"Which is perfect, because I was looking for an excuse to come back to California. I grew up in the Bay Area." I laugh nervously, for no reason.

We watch Mama Lucy silently scrape the chopped cilantro into a bowl, using her bony finger to wipe the knife clean. Finally, she looks up at us. Her eyes are a startling green. "Jay's brother lives in Oakland," Mama Lucy states. I can't tell if her tone is approving or disapproving.

Kate, undaunted, grabs the bowl in one hand and my arm in the other. "Thanks, Mama Lucy, this cilantro smells great!" she says. "C'mon, Deepti, your turn to make a pizza."

They've set up a toppings bar on the counter, small bowls filled with vegetables, sauces, cheeses. Kate uncorks the wine and pours me a glass. I spoon pesto onto a round of pizza dough, scanning the yard. I finally spot Scott in the far corner, emerging from a cluster of ferns holding a grimy tennis ball above his head. The dogs surround him, tails wagging, spittle hanging from their open mouths.

"Oh, and that's Scott," Kate says, noticing the direction of my gaze. "My brother. But you already met him."

151

Scott bounces the tennis ball hard against the patio concrete. The retriever leaps up and catches the ball in her teeth.

"I told you about what happened to him last year, right?" Kate murmurs. I make a noncommittal sound, placing pepperoni slices into an overlapping star shape on the pesto-smeared dough. "Didn't I? I thought I told you. Basically, his horrible wife left him and moved to the Netherlands, of all places. Who moves to the Netherlands? I never liked her. She used to get spray-tans every week. Orange whore. When she left he was just devastated."

We watch as Scott pets his dog's back, wrestling the mud-streaked tennis ball from her jowls.

"Are they still married?" I ask. My tongue feels dry. I sprinkle shredded cheese over the pepperoni.

"Technically they're separated. Though it's only a matter of time until the divorce papers are finalized, thank god." Kate nibbles on a piece of raw broccoli and surveys my pizza. "Looks good. I'll get Jay to come put it in the oven. He's better at it than me."

Jay is a tall, burly guy with a slight potbelly and a thick beard. I'm not physically attracted to him, but I find myself envious of Kate for being with him – not *him*, exactly, but more what he represents. Last week I was trying to describe him to my friend Bee, and all I could come up with was, "He's, like, a real grown-up. He has his shit together." I've never dated someone who has his shit together. Jay buys Kate meals and doesn't show up late for work and showers regularly and is socially aware and can make small talk. The first time we met, we chatted about the Oscar nominations and he genuinely seemed interested in my thoughts. I stand to the side as he slides my pizza into the oven's brick mouth, and he describes how the oven reaches a temperature of 750 degrees and can cook a pizza in ninety seconds. After a minute, he uses a special paddle to turn the pizza so it will cook evenly.

I watch the cheese bubble and think about how I've only dated boys, and I want to date a man. I thought Phil was a man when we started dating the second time, but as the months passed he descended back into boyhood, becoming again the entitled frat guy I'd known in college. The last time we had friends over, he ate too many pot brownies and ended the night weeping and vomiting into the toilet. I had to wipe puke off his chin with a bit of toilet paper. I want someone who will be my partner, not someone I have to take care of all the time. I want someone who will take care of me sometimes. Like Phil used to, when we first reunited in New York. Does that make me horrible?

"What do you think, Deepti?" Kate says.

"What?" Everyone is looking at me – Kate, Jay, Todd, John and Eleanor. Even Mama Lucy is peering at me from under her knit cap. I feel dazed, like I've resurfaced after being underwater.

"Should Jay sell this place and move to the beach?"

"Oh, you're moving?" I ask Jay.

"Thinking about it. There's some nice little places along the Strand." Using a long wooden paddle, he carefully extracts my pizza from the oven and slides it onto the counter.

"But then you'd lose this bad boy." I turn and there's Scott, standing right behind me – I feel my body lean slightly towards him, the hairs on our arms brushing. I'm a metal filing and he's a magnet.

Scott pats the brick wall of the pizza oven like it's one of the dogs. "You can't take this guy with you when you move."

"That's the problem," Kate says, slicing my pizza with a knife. She divvies up the slices onto paper towels and passes them around. "What do you think, Jay? Beach, or pizza oven?"

"It's a tough call," he says, and they share one of those looks, the visual equivalent of an inside joke. It's things

153

like that I find myself thinking about, late at night. Things like that I miss.

"This pizza is good," Scott says.

"Deepti made it."

"It's good," he says to me.

"Thanks." I feel myself blushing. I take a bite of my pizza and hot cheese burns the roof of my mouth.

When I left, Phil dropped to his knees and grabbed my ankles with his hands. His face was red and ugly from crying. "Wait!" he kept saying. "Let's just talk for a minute!" But we'd already talked. We'd talked and talked and talked. The only thing left to do was disengage my ankles from his clenched fingers and lug my duffel bag down to my car. He stood on the sidewalk, a helpless shell, watching me drive away. I tried not to look in my rearview mirror, but I couldn't help it. He looked small and lost. I remember the particular quality of the light, bleeding in a fragile, beautiful way through the smog-choked clouds. Driving away I felt hollow, but also relieved.

"Here, Deepti," Kate says, reaching for my hand. "I want to give you a tour of Jay's place. He spent the past year remodeling it. Wanna come, El?"

"No," Eleanor says, leaning into John's chest like a frail bird. "I'm not feeling very well." John kisses her hair and rubs her arms. I look down at my feet.

"She's totally preggers," Kate whispers to me as we cross the threshold. "Tired all the time, morning sickness, dizziness. She's terrified, though. Refuses to take a pregnancy test."

"Wow." I'm not sure what else to say. Am I supposed to wish she's pregnant? Or cross my fingers that she's not?

"Wow is right." Kate squeezes my hand. "Scott would make an amazing father, don't you think?"

Or did Kate say Jay? That would make more sense. She probably said Jay, or John – yes, John, Eleanor's husband. Not Scott. Not me.

In the kitchen, a tall man with an earring and a shaved head is pouring brownie batter into a glass pan. He looks up and smiles at us.

"Bryan! This is my friend Deepti!" Kate dances around the butcher-block island, wraps her arms around him and squeezes. "Deepti, this is the boy I had the most hopeless crush on all through high school."

"No," Bryan says, grinning. "Jared was the one you had a crush on."

Kate stiffens and pulls away from him. I can't quite read her expression. I've never heard her mention anyone named Jared.

"Hey, hey," Bryan says, reaching for her. "I'm sorry, I forgot. He was my best friend back then, it's only natural for me to bring him up sometimes."

She doesn't say anything. She looks down at the granite countertop, her brow wrinkled.

I'm about to ask who Jared is when Bryan addresses me, his tone teasing, obviously trying to lighten the mood. "What can I say, Deepti?" His eyes are on Kate. "I had perfectly gelled hair and a puka shell necklace. Katie stood no chance."

After a moment Kate smiles, running her finger through the slick of batter left in the bowl. "All the girls were in love with you," she admits. "But can you believe it, Deepti? Out of everyone, he chose *me* for his Prom date."

"You were stunning. Remember that red dress?"

"Sweetheart neckline," Kate describes. "Little cap sleeves. Flounce skirt. I felt like a princess in that dress. Meanwhile, Bryan was making eyes at Diana Wheeler's date all night. What was his name?"

"Phil something," he says. Inwardly, I wince.

"But I was the one who got to slow-dance with you. All the other girls were so jealous. Listen, Deepti – he was THE most popular guy in school."

"You're the only one I'm still in touch with." Bryan slides the pan into the oven and winks at me, jerking his

155

thumb at Kate. "This girl came to every single one of my chemo treatments. She'd sit in the chair next to me and read *Harry Potter* out loud."

"At first he teased me about bringing him *children's* books," Kate explains. "But soon he was hooked. Weren't you?"

"I was."

"He was convinced Harry and Ron are secret lovers." Kate rolls her eyes.

"What do you mean 'was'? I'm still convinced! They're just like Todd and me."

I laugh. Kate holds the batter-smeared bowl in my direction, but I shake my head. She rinses it in the sink. "Speaking of your boyfriend, Bry, I think you'd better go save him. Jay's been talking his ear off about the science of brewing beer."

Bryan sets the oven timer. "I'll see you two out there. It was nice to meet you, Deepti."

Bryan ambles out to the backyard. I watch the light glint off his shiny shaved head and reconfigure my first impression. *Chemo. Cancer. Not choice.*

"He had the most beautiful hair," Kate says, as if reading my thoughts. "He used to spend all weekend surfing, and his hair would get so blonde from the sun." She sets the bowl on the dish-rack and dries her hands on a towel.

"So he doesn't surf anymore?"

"Oh no, he goes all the time. But I just meant his hair. He had brain cancer, and there's a patch of his hair that is never going to grow back. From the drugs, I guess. So now he just shaves his whole head."

Brain cancer. I'm not sure what type of cancer I was expecting, but certainly not that. I ask if he's in remission now.

"It's been maybe eight, nine years? Yeah, Bry's amazing. The prognosis was not good. His boyfriend left him – said he couldn't deal with it. What an asshole."

I picture Kate sitting next to Bryan in a sterile hospital room, reading about magic in her sure, soothing voice. Something about it makes me feel unglued. I bite the inside of my cheek.

"But Bryan beat it," Kate says. "And then he met Todd, and I've never seen him happier." She reaches forward and plucks something from my hair – a jacaranda blossom. She drops it into the trash. "The body is an incredible thing, you know? Our ability to heal."

I nod, thinking about my first date with Phil back in college. The happiness I felt sitting across that sticky table from him at The Grove, the two of us eating terrible Chinese food and pretending to have deep, grown-up conversations. Such hope I had back then. What a miracle love seemed to be. The way it expanded in my chest, crowding out the worry for a little while.

Kate leads me on the promised house tour, through the dining area and living room, Jay's home office and the guest bedroom. The walls are painted bright colors and there are lots of mirrors and throw pillows and cozy folded blankets. It is not the bachelor pad I was expecting.

"Jay redid the whole place, after his ex-wife moved out," Kate says. "I helped some.
I told Jay we could make it feel like home again. But he's still talking about moving. Even with the redecorating, this place has a lot of painful memories."

"I didn't realize he was married before."

"Oh yeah, just for a couple years. She was horrible. She cheated on him all the time. He still has some trust issues, but we're working through it."

In the master bedroom a wide, gauzy-curtained window looks out at the trees, a dim blur of branches in the twilight. The bedroom I shared with Phil was cluttered with framed photos and books and random knick-knacks: a mostly intact sand dollar from our trip to Florida, a Snoopy figurine I fell in love with at a thrift store, a glass Coke bottle filled with pennies.

I excuse myself to go to the bathroom. Kate, perhaps sensing my mood, says she'll meet me outside. And so here I am, standing in front of the gilded bathroom mirror, watching myself cry. I imagine Phil doing what Jay has done – removing all traces of me from our apartment – and I don't know what to feel. It's not like I want him to keep the apartment exactly as it was. Except, that *is* what I want. I want him to move on but I want a part of him to miss me forever. I blow my nose again and again. I splash water on my face. It's things like this I find myself thinking about, late at night: all the gathered-up minutiae from my life that I left behind, irretrievable.

When I make my way back outside, everyone has gathered around the fire pit. I sit down next to Scott. Mama Lucy is telling a story about Jay as a boy, throwing a tantrum at the grocery store, knocking an entire row of cereal boxes onto the floor. "It was all because I wouldn't get you that toy you wanted. What was it?" she asks.

"The Ghostbusters toilet action figure," Jay says. "What? Back me up, guys – Bry, John – it was cool, right?"

Everyone's shaking their heads, grinning. Mama Lucy slaps her knee. "Oh god, all that trouble for a *toilet!*" she exclaims. Her laughter is surprisingly girlish.

Conversation turns to another friend I haven't met, Emily, who is getting married next month. I settle back and listen. The fire is soothing and I realize I'm happy to be sitting here, part of this laughing group of people, instead of alone in my apartment. Bryan emerges from the house wearing oven mitts, carrying the glass pan of brownies. Scott hands me a warm square of brownie on a paper napkin.

"Are these…pot brownies?" I whisper.

Scott shakes his head. "No, we wouldn't dare with Mama Lucy around."

We look at her. She's hunched in a woven blanket, her face younger-looking in the warm glow of the fire. "Are you kidding?" I smile, feeling bold, the wine loosening my thoughts. "Look at that hat. She was a total hippie stoner, back in the day."

Scott laughs so hard he nearly chokes on his brownie. I flush with pleasure.

"No, listen," he says when he regains himself. "Bryan makes the best brownies because dumps like two bags of chocolate chips in the batter. You're basically eating a melted chocolate bar."

His dog trots over, her muzzle flecked with dirt and mud, tennis ball abandoned in some pocket of the yard. I scratch behind her ears. Scott runs his hand along her spine, smiling. I wonder if people were surprised when his wife left him. Or maybe they saw it coming. Maybe he saw it coming. I mean, he doesn't look like a broken man. He looks the way I feel: sleepily content from the wine and the food. Still, Kate's words run through my head. *When she left he was just devastated.*

When I left, before Phil dropped to his knees and grabbed my ankles and begged me not to go, he gripped my bare shoulders, hard, in his hands. And I felt scared of him.

"I'm scared of you," I said.

That's when his face crumpled and he began to cry.

That's when I realized meant it. I *was* scared of him, truly, and we had reached the breaking point. My fear eclipsing my love.

I even glanced in my rearview to make sure he wasn't following me. He wasn't. He just stood there, arms limp at his sides, a crying figure growing steadily smaller. I didn't cry until weeks later, when I arrived for my new job in California, and the fog sank down into the purple hills, and I was alone.

Sometimes now I wonder if I was silly to be scared. He never hurt me. He never hit me. He got angry sometimes and yelled and threw things across the room, but never at me. But my shoulders were red from the grip of his fingers. I dreamed again and again of his eyes, flashing with anger, and woke with my fists clenched.

159

That was why, when I saw a flyer for a free yoga class at the rec center, I decided to go. I'd never done yoga before, but I thought it might help.

I watch the dog set her chin on Scott's leg, sniffing at his brownie. "Chocolate's not good for you," he says, holding the brownie above her head. I polish off my last bite and crumple the napkin in my palm. Across the fire, Mama Lucy has fallen asleep, head listing to the side. Kate is sitting on Jay's lap, Bryan on Todd's. John and Eleanor are lying somewhere in the grass together.

My arms are goosepimpled and I realize I'm staring at Scott's hooded sweatshirt, imagining it wrapped around me. I want him to unzip it and usher me into the warmth of his chest, zipping it back up around the both of us. I imagine the scent of his skin, cologne mixed with sweat. I imagine my lips grazing his neck, wonder if he would taste of salt or soap, or maybe both.

When I got back together with Phil in New York, I was drunk. We met for a let's-catch-up drink that turned into two friendly drinks, then three *very* friendly drinks. I was a lightweight – still am – and my drunken self decided I wanted him back. He called a cab from the bar and rode home with me, helped me out of the cab and made sure I found my keys, but he wouldn't come up to my apartment. He told me later he didn't want things between us to restart that way. I leaned forward and kissed him quickly before stumbling up the front steps. I remember waving to him from my open doorway. Or maybe I don't really remember; maybe it's a memory I've created – that he waited to make sure I got inside safely before turning and disappearing down the block. Back then he used to walk all around the city. It was a point of pride for him not to take the subway. In my memory, I waved to him from the doorway and he winked at me before turning and walking away. Part of me thought that I would never see him again. The other part of me felt sure that he would always keep me safe.

Both parts of me were wrong.

Still, I can't help listening to my inner voice that keeps insisting, *Maybe this one will be different from all the others before.*

Abruptly Scott stands up and begins gathering plates and wineglasses.

"Leave it!" Kate says, yawning.

He waves her words away. "I'm happy to do the dishes. Besides, I don't want Blue to break anything."

I pat the dog's head and her tail thumps against the grass.

"You wanna come?" Scott asks me in a quiet voice.

Feeling like an extra slipping offstage before the play is over, I grip a bouquet of wineglasses in one hand, a stack of plates in the other. I wonder if the others are watching us, if they notice our elbows gently touching as we make our way across the patio. The wineglasses clink in my fingers. Under our feet, crushed jacaranda blossoms smear the concrete.

I think of Scott's ex, packing her suitcase, preparing to uproot her life. I think of Phil, standing hunched and alone on the sidewalk. Sometimes the world seems like nothing more than a giant mess we are all haphazardly making and then attempting to clean up for each other.

And yet. Here I am, walking with Scott towards the light blazing from the kitchen window. He glances at me, opens his mouth to say something. I smile back, preparing to listen. I try to hold the breakable things steady in my hands.

Woman, Running Late, in a Dress

A woman is running late for her doctor's appointment. A voice asks her to hold the elevator, and she believes in karma, so she does. A man steps in. He presses the button for the third floor. "You're welcome," he says, then plunges a knife into her arm.
What color is the woman's dress?

Dr. Breen was telling the riddle. He never mentioned a dress. I'm certain he didn't. He only said "a woman" – he didn't describe what she was wearing.

Or maybe I'm remembering wrong. Maybe he did mention a dress, at the beginning? And I simply wasn't paying close enough attention? Perhaps the trick of the riddle is that people get so swept up in the glamour and surprise of the violence that they forget everything else.

The next few moments coalesced into a blur. Gasps and shouts, a hand on my arm, sequined gowns and expensive colognes parting before me. And then, there, Raymond's crumpled form on the hardwood floor of the foyer, like a sleeve torn from a jacket, the stitches frayed and useless.

I never found out the answer.

What color? What color is her dress?

Maybe she doesn't believe in karma. Maybe she's just a benevolent woman. The type of person who holds elevator doors open for other people because it's the right thing to do, not because she expects to be rewarded for it later by the cosmic justice of the universe.

Raymond is – was – a general surgeon in the E.R. The party that night was a benefit for the hospital. We argued about where to park.

"Why don't you turn – oh, now you've missed it. There was a perfect spot in that row."

"Carol, I hate when you do this."

"What? I'm just trying to help – "

"I'm the one driving. I can make a decision myself."

I folded my arms against my chest. The clasp on my clutch caught at the fabric of my dress. "I just thought it'd be best to park by the elevators."

"Why does it matter?"

"You know I hate to walk in heels."

"But those spots are too small for this car."

"Well, then we could park valet. Why don't we park valet?"

"Carol," Raymond sighed. "Why does everything have to be an argument?"

"We're not arguing, we're discussing."

"Everything has to be so difficult."

"I guess I just know what I like."

"Well, damn it, Carol," Raymond said. "It gets tiring." His tone of voice was like steel wool on bare skin.

We ended up parking halfway between the elevators and the far wall. I kept my arms crossed, teetering unsteadily in my high heels without taking Raymond's arm. At one time our bodies had drifted towards each other as if twin magnets were embedded beneath our skin. Now I have weak ankles and no magnetic energy. When Raymond held the vestibule door open for me, I nodded thanks but did not meet his eyes.

Later, at the seafood buffet, he started talking to Susanne Anderson, so I struck up a conversation with Dr. Breen. I laughed at his jokes, touching his shoulder lightly with my fingers. I wanted Raymond to see. I thought I would wait until the dancing started to make amends. And then Dr. Breen turned to me and said, "Do you like riddles?"

Marie Vindraire is running late for her appointment. But when a voice says, "Hold the doors, will ya!" she sighs and presses the elevator's "Open Door" button.

A man steps in. "Thanks," he says with a smile. He presses the button for the third floor. Then he turns to face her, and, still smiling, says, "You're welcome, my dear," before plunging a knife into her left arm.

Her dress is stained with blood.

He must have said the answer straight out, and I wasn't paying attention. That's the kicker. He must have said it at the very beginning, right after he said, "Listen carefully." I nodded my head and smiled, but I didn't listen carefully.

"Listen to me, Carol," Raymond muttered once. I was halfway out of the room but his tone of voice was one I hadn't heard in a long time. Not quite desperate, but there was desperation mixed in. Fear, too. The same tone his voice had taken when he first told me he loved me, thirty-three years ago at a rest stop near the Pennsylvania border after our first weekend away together. We were sitting on a picnic bench eating cheese-and-tomato sandwiches. When he told me, I was so surprised I let go of my paper napkin and it blew away.

So I turned, when I heard his tone. Raymond sat on the edge of our bed, the dying sun slanting through the blinds, making him squint. "You never listen," he said. "I'm trying to tell you something."

Actually, that is not what happened. This is what happened:

"Listen to me, Carol," Raymond muttered. I was halfway out of the room, so I did not turn. Instead, I went into the kitchen and peeled potatoes for dinner. I imagine the sunlight shone weakly through the tilted blinds, casting soft stripes on his face. But I did not look back, so it is only imagining. Perhaps the blinds were shut entirely.

Funny, how colors are associated with emotion. Green means envy. Blue means peace. When she was a girl, Marie Vindraire's mother painted her bedroom walls eggplant purple, because she said Marie was her princess, and purple means royalty. Marie loved her mother very much.

Maybe her dress is red. For love.

Or red for hate.

Or both.

Raymond and I met on a blind date set up by Penny Saramond, my sorority sister and the girlfriend of Raymond's friend Tom. We were to meet at a café downtown, and I was running late. I blamed the rain, and the traffic, but really it was because I changed outfits a dozen times. That was my year of profound anxiety. All my stockings had runs. My lipstick smudged easily. I had taken to triple-checking things: that the iron was off, that the door was locked, that I had both earrings on and necklace securely clasped. I finally left the house wearing a gray dress from my roommate's closet.

My eyes are a deep slate gray, almost blue.

When I arrived at the café, Raymond was sitting at a table by the window, gazing outside at the dripping, rain-glossed city. I thought it was him – he had dark hair and a pale complexion as Penny had described – and when he glanced up and saw me and smiled, I hoped it was him. We sat at the table by the window for three hours, as the sun gradually poked holes in the rainclouds.

"I remember the first time I saw you," Raymond told me years later. "You sparkled in that gray dress."

I wish I could remember what color Raymond was wearing that day, the day he and I began. But I can't.

The man says, "You're welcome" as he plunges the knife into her arm. Why? What does the woman have to thank him for?

"You're still dwelling on that riddle?" Sylvie asks. We're having lunch at The Basil Leaf Café, sitting at the outside patio enclosed by potted palms. They bend in the breeze, leaning in slightly towards us, and then away as if they've been caught eavesdropping.

"I've been thinking…" I stir my chicken-and-rice soup and watch the steam escape from the surface, dissolving into the breeze. "Maybe there's something wrong with her arm."

"Whose arm?"

"Marie. The woman he stabs in the elevator. Or else why would he say 'You're welcome' before he stabs her?"

Sylvie takes a bite of her sandwich, wiping stray avocado from her mouth with a napkin. She looks off into the distance while she chews. I like Sylvie because she understands my life, but is also removed from it. She was married to William for eighteen years – that's when I met her, in a community college class, and we became friends – but six years ago she divorced him to marry Josh, a boyish nonprofit worker ten years younger than she is. Sylvie's like that. She believes in blind, fierce, aching love.

Sylvie swallows. "I don't know," she says. "Maybe he's just a raving lunatic."

"Sylvie!"

"What? *He's* what's wrong with her arm. He stabs her, for godsake."

"I just hate...not knowing."

She leans closer to me. "Honey, I worry about you. You're getting so hung up on this riddle..." She reaches for my hand and squeezes it. "The longer you push real life away, the harder it's gonna be."

I look down into my soup. The grains of rice clump together. I stir them apart.

"Can people get tumors in their arms?" I ask.

Tumors. Cancer. Bone cancer, maybe. Or leukemia. The knife wound bleeds like crazy and Marie Vindraire faints and they find out she has leukemia. Doctors wouldn't have known about it, but they tend to her wound and do some tests and catch it early, before the typical symptoms present themselves. So they treat it early and she survives, and it's all thanks to the man who stabbed her in the elevator.

When I am alone, late at night, and I cannot sleep, and the jacaranda branches slap against the side of the house like a wild heartbeat, sometimes I think about it. I bargain retrospectively for time; I play What If. What If we go back and erase the argument in the car? What If I take his arm while we walk to the elevator? What If I never hear Dr. Breen's asinine riddle because I am talking to Raymond instead, am there beside him when he slumps to the ground, face drained of color?

Raymond was only fifty-eight. I thought apologies could wait until the dancing started.

I wonder, if he had survived the heart attack that night, if maybe it would have brought us together again.

Perhaps the man is not really a man, but an angel. He says, "You're welcome" because he is saving Marie Vindraire. God told him to get in an elevator with a woman in a dress, a certain-colored dress, and plunge a knife into her left arm – just deep enough, but not too deep. But he needs to know what color the woman's dress is. What color is he looking for? This is crucial. Without the dress, everything collapses.

It is said that tragedy either pulls two people closer together or pushes them apart. When Raymond's brother died – suicide – we had been married only three years. At the time I thought the tragedy brought us closer. I held him when he cried. I sat beside him at the funeral, stiff-backed, our sweaty palms clasped together. He gripped my hand so tightly. I felt strong, impregnable, like I was the only thing keeping him upright. At the wake, I helped his mother in the kitchen, cutting cucumber sandwiches into triangles and pouring sweet tea into paper cups.

I was impregnable, and then I was pregnant. I took the test right there in the drugstore bathroom stall, two weeks to the day after the funeral. The fragile blue line in that tiny plastic window both thrilled and terrified me in a way I have never felt before or since.

Raymond seemed surprised, but happy. He picked me up and kissed me; he danced me around the kitchen. He might have been putting it all on, a show of giddiness for my benefit alone, but I didn't see that at the time. I only saw his smile. I only heard the words he told me.

"This is wonderful, Carol," he said.

"I couldn't be more excited," he said.

"My beautiful wife," he said. "My beautiful pregnant wife. I'll feed you ice cream and pancakes. I'll buy you pastrami sandwiches at one in the morning. Just say what you need, anything you need, and your dashing husband will get it for you."

I laughed and kissed him. In that moment, I was happy.

Marie Vindraire wakes up in a hospital room with striped wallpaper and sterile medicine smells. Her daughter is holding her hand.

Marie is surprised, because they've been fighting lately. Her daughter moved out a few weeks ago, throwing phrases at Marie over her shoulder: I hate you, I hate you, you don't understand, I'm moving in with Sarah. Marie missed her daughter terribly. They hadn't talked in days. Now, her daughter smiles at Marie and squeezes her hand. There are tears in her eyes.

"I was worried, Mom," she says. "I'm so glad you're gonna be okay."

Marie is grateful to the man in the elevator, because he brought them together again.

We lost the baby at a routine appointment on a Wednesday afternoon. The ultrasound technician couldn't find a heartbeat. I went to the appointment by myself; Raymond was overwhelmed with paperwork that day, so I told him he didn't have to come. The technician called the doctor, and the doctor called Raymond's office. I sat on the exam table waiting for them. My growing belly was smeared with ultrasound gel and the metal table was sharply cold against my bare thighs. When Raymond finally stepped into the room, his face drawn and his tie askew, I knew with weary certainty that the baby was a dead weight inside me. I lifted myself down from the table and reached for Raymond, but I stumbled and fell, and he was not quick enough to catch me.

I came home that evening with an empty cocoon and tender bruises on my eye, my forehead, my shoulder.

"It'll be okay," Raymond said, over and over again. "We'll be okay, Carol. I'm here." He gently kissed my bruises, but they lingered for days without fading.

Marie Vindraire wakes up in a hospital room with striped wallpaper and sterile medicine smells. Her husband is holding her hand.

She is surprised, because they've been fighting fiercely lately. He moved out a few weeks ago, throwing words at her over his shoulder: trial separation, divorce, growing apart, different people. She missed him terribly. They hadn't talked in days. Now, he smiles at her and kisses her forehead. There are tears in his eyes.

"I was worried," he says. "I'm so glad you're going to be okay."

Marie is grateful to the man in the elevator, because he brought them together again.

Nine months ago, a young teacher hung himself and it was all over the local news. We had dinner with friends the evening after. Raymond, claiming a headache, asked if we could reschedule, but we had already rescheduled once.

"We're all so busy, Ray," I said. "You know how it is – if we cancel now, it'll be months before we see them. And it would be rude on such short notice, don't you think?"

We were barely through the appetizers before routine small talk waned to the news, and the news digressed to the suicide.

"Supposedly everyone who knew him was surprised," Margaret said. "His students – middle schoolers, I think, weren't they Jack? – well, anyway, they all simply adored him, it sounds like."

"My brother committed suicide," Raymond said softly. He stabbed a scallop with his fork. "It was the hardest thing I ever went through."

He hadn't talked about his brother's death for years. I reached under the table for his hand, but I couldn't find it so I patted his knee instead. Jack groped awkwardly for words; Margaret murmured sympathy, but from the way she leaned forward in her chair I could tell she wanted to hear all the details. I wished we had stayed home.

Driving away from the restaurant, it started to rain, and Raymond focused his attention on chasing raindrops from the windshield with the slow, squeaky wipers.

"If you want to talk about it, I'm here," I said.

Raymond didn't answer. I thought perhaps he hadn't heard. Rain drummed on the roof, making me feel claustrophobic. Outside, colors blurred and smeared together.

"You didn't know him," Raymond said.

"What?"

"You didn't know him. You only met him once."

It was true. The first and last time I saw his brother was our wedding day. Tall, thin, with Raymond's dark hair and their mother's easy smile. He drank too much at the wedding reception, but he was so charming that nobody said anything. He asked me to dance to a Frank Sinatra song, I can't remember which one, but I do remember how close he held me, the way I could feel the rise and fall of his chest against my own. When the song finished, he kissed me wetly to the side of my mouth – he may have been aiming for my cheek, or he may have been aiming for my lips – and whispered, "Ray's the best guy I know. Take care of him, will you?" Then he turned and wandered away from me through the crowd of dancing bodies. And then he shot himself in his backyard on a blue-skied Sunday morning, under an apple tree just beginning to blossom.

Later, looking back, Marie will not be able to recall the man's height or weight, his eyes or nose or even his hair color, but she will remember his presence, the feeling of warm wholeness that overcame her even as the knife plunged into her arm with shocking, biting pain.

Does it matter what color her dress is?

I sit on the floor in our bedroom, my face pressed against the soft cotton T-shirt Raymond last slept in. The riddle loops through my mind on repeat.

A woman is running late for her doctor's appointment. A voice asks her to hold the elevator…

I close my eyes and imagine myself back at the party that night, talking to Dr. Breen. I can see his face clearly in my memory, his trim mustache and wire-rimmed glasses.

She believes in karma, so she does…

I am holding a glass of Merlot, nearly empty. I touch Dr. Breen's shoulder with my right hand. I laugh, tilting my head back, but I glance around the room for Raymond. I want Raymond to be watching. I want Raymond to be jealous.

A man steps in…

Raymond is a few feet away, talking to Susanne Anderson, a general practitioner whose office is next-door to his. She is wearing a dark green evening gown, her hair coiled in an elaborate knot. She has never been friendly to me but has always been especially friendly to Raymond. I am upset he is talking to her. I look away. I touch Dr. Breen's arm again. I laugh so hard I gasp for breath.

He presses the button for the third floor…

Dr. Breen leans in. His breath is warm and smells of bourbon. According to Sylvie, he and his wife recently filed for divorce. "Do you like riddles?" he asks.

"Yes, of course I do," I say. I smile.

He smiles back, leaning even closer, his palm on my back. "Listen carefully…"

"You're welcome," the man says, then plunges a knife into her arm…

I nod. But I am distracted. I am looking around for Raymond, but he is nowhere to be seen. And neither is Susanne.

What color is the woman's dress?

And suddenly, sitting in the bedroom with Raymond's shirt in the gathering dark, I remember: "Listen carefully," Dr. Breen says. "Imagine you are this young woman. A woman running late for her doctor's appointment."

It's me. That's the riddle. I am the woman running late in a dress.

The dress I wore to the ball was made of shiny silken fabric the color of my eyes. Steel gray, almost blue. When I had slipped it over my head I had felt young again – like I was getting ready for the Prom, anticipating my first kiss. Filled with foolish, beautiful hopes.

That evening, I had stepped out into the hall, the dress swishing softly against my legs. Raymond was on the couch, reading the newspaper while he waited for me to finish getting ready. In that moment, he was a stranger to me again. I felt shy and nervous, watching him. His dark hair had turned gray, but it was as if I was standing again at the doorway of that downtown café on a rainy afternoon, yearning for a future I could grasp tightly with both hands. I had hesitated, watching him, wondering if he was the one I was supposed to meet.

He looked up and saw me. A wide smile spread across his face. And I walked towards him, knowing with foolish, beautiful certainty that he was.

"Carol," Raymond said, putting the newspaper down and lifting himself up from the couch. We stood there, facing each other. Nerves fluttered inside me. I felt like I was standing at a precipice, afraid to look over the edge, not knowing what lay below. Then Raymond reached for my hand.

"Carol," he said softly, "you sparkle in that gray dress."

About the Author

Dallas Woodburn, a recent Steinbeck Fellow in Creative Writing at San Jose State University, received her MFA in Fiction from Purdue University and her BA in Creative Writing from the University of Southern California. Her writing has appeared in a number of journals, magazines, newspapers, and anthologies. A three-time Pushcart Prize nominee, she won first place in the international Glass Woman Prize and second place in the American Fiction Prize. She is the founder of Write On! Books, an organization that empowers young people through reading and writing endeavors: www.writeonbooks.org.

ACKNOWLEDGEMENTS

First, huge thanks to J. Bruce Fuller and W. Scott Thomason for bringing this book into the world. I am so grateful for J's gorgeous cover design and Scott's astute, careful edits of every page. It has been a dream-come-true to join the Yellow Flag Press family!

Thank you to Beatrice Murch for letting us use her gorgeous photograph for the cover, and to Jeffrey Dransfeldt for taking such lovely headshots for me.

Thank you to the Martha Heasley Cox Center for Steinbeck Studies at San Jose State University for supporting my work. Many of these stories were birthed and edited during my year as a Steinbeck Fellow, and the insightful feedback of Vanessa Hua, Tommy Mouton and Paul Douglass improved the manuscript immensely. Thanks also to Nick Taylor, Director of the Steinbeck Center, for his continued encouragement.

I first envisioned writing a linked short story collection during my time as an MFA student at Purdue University, in large part due to wonderful professors who introduced me to collections like Jennifer Egan's *A Visit from the Goon Squad* and Elizabeth Strout's *Olive Kitteridge*. Thank you to my professors Porter Shreve, Bich Minh Nguyen, Sharon Solwitz and Patricia Henley. Special thanks to Shavonne Clarke, Natalie van Hoose, Tiffany Chiang, Terrance Manning, Mike Campbell, Kelsey Ronan, and Alisha Karabinus – all writers I admire, who I am fortunate to also consider friends. Big thanks and love to Chidelia Edochie, my friend from the moment we met, whose daring prose continually inspires me and whose voice I hear in my head, cheering me on when I doubt myself.

Thank you to the Creative Writing program at the University of Southern California for helping me build a daily writing routine and find my voice. Special thanks to professors James Ragan, Susan Segal and Richard Fliegel for nurturing my confidence; Viet Thahn Nguyen for expanding my worldview and providing superb feedback for numerous drafts of "Three Sundays at The Grove"; and Aimee Bender for being my role model as a writer, teacher and human being. Thanks also to Trezza Azzopardi at the University of East Anglia in Norwich, England, where I spent an influential semester studying creative writing. At USC, I was fortunate to take classes alongside Tera Ragan, Janet Thielke, Stuart Rodriguez and Schaeffer Nelson – fellow writers and friends who pushed me to grow.

Thank you to the Key West Literary Seminar for sweeping me out of a Midwestern January and into paradise for a week of writing! Special thanks to Hilma Wolitzer's fiction workshop, and especially to Leigh Camacho Rourks and Sharon Harrigan who have become two of my favorite writers and online friends. My biggest thanks to Key West is for rooming me with amazing poet and essayist Carand Burnet, who has become a dear friend.

Thank you to Murphy Writing of Stockton University for generously supporting my work with the Jan-ai Scholarship to attend the Winter Poetry & Prose Getaway, which came as a huge creative boost exactly when I needed it. Thank you to Peter Murphy, Amanda Murphy, Cynthia Walker, and everyone in Michelle Cameron's fiction workshop.

Thank you to the editors of the anthologies and journals who first published these stories, whose meticulous edits made each piece much better than I could have on my own.

Thank you to all of my teachers, classmates and friends from elementary school onward who have encouraged my writing over the years. Too many to name, but you know who you are!

Thank you to my students, who continually remind me of the joy and magic that comes from unleashing words onto the blank page.

Thank you to Grandma and Grandpap for the "writing retreat" – one year that stretched into nearly three. I am grateful for all the stories, laughter, shared meals, and giant mugs of tea gone cold on the counter. I treasure you both more than words can express!

Thank you to my family and to friends who have become family. My in-laws: Barbara, Allyn, Laurel, Allyson, Colin, and Charlotte; my Gramps; all of my aunts, uncles and cousins (special shout-out to Mary, Annie, and Arianna); and my dear friends Erica, Dana, Laur, Mikey, Ben, Justin, Fawn, Ken, Kathy, Alicia, Tania, Henry, Joan, Annette and Ron. And a big thank-you hug to Holly for being my first reader/cheerleader, for celebrating with glitter cards and baked goods, for knowing when to share her wisdom and when to simply listen.

Thank you to my dad, Woody – my all-time favorite writer – for his contagious positivity and unending encouragement, for all of our talks about characters and plot and ideas, and for always making me feel like a best-selling author. Thank you to my beautiful mom, Lisa, for giving me her kindness and strength, for her listening ear, for our many walks and adventures. Thank you to my younger brother, Greg – my "twin" since the day he was born – for always saying he is proud of me, and for inspiring me to be my best self while also giving myself grace.

And thank you, finally, to Allyn, for making me believe – for showing me every day – that stories can indeed have happy endings.

D.W.
March 2018

Some of the stories in this collection originally appeared in slightly different versions in the following magazines and anthologies, to whose editors grateful acknowledgement is made: "Near-Death Experience" in *Conclave: A Journal of Character*; "Numb" in *Monkeybicycle*; "Slowly, Slowly Without Much Notice" in *Inscape Literary Magazine* and *Embers & Flames* (Outrider Press); "Jared Sampson's Mom" in *The Valparaiso Fiction Review*; "Three Sundays at The Grove" in *The East Bay Review* and *Not Somewhere Else But Here: A Contemporary Anthology of Women & Place* (Sundress Publications); "The Stars in Illinois" in *The Nashville Review*; "Living Alone" in *Louisiana Literature* and *Steinbeck Now*; "Specks of Dust in Sunlight" in *Zyzzyva*; "Hearts Like Lemons in Fists of Dew" in *American Fiction 13: The Best Unpublished Short Stories by Emerging American Writers* (New Rivers Press); "Under the Jacaranda Trees" in *Prism Review*; "Woman, Running Late, in a Dress" in *Arcadia Magazine* and *Sequestrum Magazine*.

CPSIA information can be obtained
at www.ICGtesting.com
Printed in the USA
LVHW01s2325050918
589315LV00001B/90/P

9 781387 571215